The Cattlemen

By

Bill Shuey

Adrinne,
Best Wishes
Bill Shuey
10/2022

Bill Shuey

The Cattlemen

The Cattlemen

All Rights Reserved Worldwide
Copyright 2019 Bill Shuey

ISBN 13: 978-1724686794
ISBN 10: 1724686798

1st Revision February 2019
2nd Revision December 2019

Printed in the United States of America

Acknowledgements

Many thanks to my sister-in-law, Bern, who proof reads my books and articles without compensation and lends her time to my literary efforts without complaint.

And to my brother Ken, who designs my cover art work for the same compensation as his wife.

And to Marisa Mott www.cowboykimono.com who did the final artwork and wrap on the book.

And a special thanks to April Wade the newest member of the team, who did the final proof on the finished book.

And to my wife, Gloria, who had encouraged me for years to author books of fiction and now suffers my time consuming effort of getting them on paper and in print.

Dedication

This western yarn is dedicated to my late father, Claude E. Shuey, who loved the west and western novels. Hopefully, he would find this effort interesting.

Cattlemen – Persons who breed, rear, or tend cattle, or raise cattle on a large scale, usually for beef, especially the owners of a cattle ranch.

Chapter 1

James Budwell (Bud) Baxter was a long drink of water, about 6' 4" tall and extremely thin. Bud was the type of person who would have to stand in the same place twice just to cast a shadow. He had rusty red hair, a large mustache, and a scar above his left eye from a musket ball which grazed him in a hunting accident. Bud was gregarious and met mighty few strangers. Having a conversation with Bud wasn't much of a problem because he would do most of the talking.

William Travis (Bill) Brubaker was Bud's polar opposite in many ways. Bill was also tall, 6'0'in his stocking feet, but there the comparison ended. He had dark brown hair and wore it shoulder length and kept a well-trimmed Van Dyke beard. Bill was quiet and introspective and rarely commented on anything without giving it due consideration and factoring in the implications. As much as Bud was willing to talk, Bill was more inclined to listen and liked to say, "You can't get in much trouble listening."

Bud and Bill were both born on the same day in 1840, Bud was born at 10:00 PM, and Bill shortly before 11:00 PM on July 7. Both men would joke they had never been more than one hour apart their entire life. Both men were born and grew up on farms in Crawford County, Missouri, in an area now known as the Huzzah Valley. Both the Baxter and Brubaker families owned fairly large farms near the confluence of the Courtois and Meramec Rivers. The bottom land soil was rich and afforded excellent permanent pasture for grazing cattle.

Bud and Bill wanted to be cowboys. They had read the Saint Louis Dispatch which carried stories about Indians and cattle drives in Texas. They devoured penny novels about the west, gunslingers, cattlemen, and Indians and wanted to be a part of the lifestyle. Both young men thought they knew cattle because both farms raised mixed breed Hereford beef cattle. The purebred Hereford originated in Herefordshire in the West Midlands of England and was first brought to America in 1817 when Henry Clay brought a cow, a heifer, and a young bull to his Kentucky farm. The Baxter and Brubaker cattle were distant descendants of those cattle. Once Bud and Bill made it to the west and had to deal with Texas Longhorn cattle, they were to realize they didn't know beans about cows.

****

The elder Baxter and Brubaker knew their sons were going to be headed out for the west and adventure sooner rather than later. On their birthday in 1858, both fathers gave their sons Colt Paterson .36 caliber revolvers and ten inch Bowie knives the local blacksmith, who was accomplished at making blades, made for them. Both young men knew they would need a rifle to hunt game and protect themselves at greater distances than a pistol could provide. Both men worked part-time on other farms and saved every penny they were paid. In 1857, both young men had taken part of their savings and rode the forty mile trip to Pacific, Missouri, to Bradford's Gun Shop and purchased two of the second model 1851 Sharps rifle. The rifle shot the .52 caliber cartridge and fired a 475 grain projectile. The Sharps rifle they purchased was manufactured by the Robbins & Lawrence Company of Windsor, Vermont, which developed the weapon for mass production.

In August of 1858, Bud and Bill were at the Meramec Saloon and Eatery in Steeleville, Missouri, when one of the Nuence men made a loud and disparaging remark about Bill's younger sister Mae. Bill turned and looked at the man and said "Fid Nuence, you need to take that lie back."

Nuence looked at him and said, "Or what, Sonny?"

"Or I will beat the snot out of you."

Nuence pulled out an Arkansas Toothpick and said, "I think I'll just see what you had for breakfast, boy." Bill had a decision to make. He could pull his pistol and shoot the man, turn tail, or pull his own knife. He decided it was as good a day as any to find out what he was made of, so he pulled out his Bowie.

Nuence feinted to his left and thrust with his knife. Bill sidestepped and circled to his left. Nuence feinted again and then came forward and thrust again. Bill sidestepped again and flicked his blade and brought blood on Nuence's right shoulder. Bill said, "I brought blood. Just apologize before this gets worse." Nuence was now in a rage and charged. Bill sidestepped again and put a sizable gash in the man's right buttock. Bill said, "One last time, Nuence. You have been drinking, and you are too slow. Just apologize and go home." Nuence charged in again. Brubaker caught the man's wrist and buried his Bowie in the man's brisket puncturing the left lung and causing massive bleeding.

Bill had done nothing more than defend himself, but the hills around the Huzzah were filled with Nuences who were clannish people. It was a certainty he couldn't beat them all with guns or knives. As Brubaker left the saloon, he looked at Bud and said, "I think it is time for me to head west; it would probably be best for my health."

Bill went to the farm, told his father what had happened, and began packing his haversack. His mother brought him some jerked meat, cold biscuits, a small skillet, an old pot to brew coffee, and enough Arbuckle to make two – three pots depending on how strong he wanted the brew. He packed his slicker, ground cover, and blanket on his chestnut gelding. Bill hugged his mother and siblings and shook hands with his father. Bill's father looked at him and said, "When you are ready to start your ranch let me know, and I will send you a Hereford bull and heifer to start your breeding stock."

Bill turned Sonny, his gelding horse and started down the lane leading away from the farm house and was met by Bud Baker riding up on a dun colored mare. Bud said, "Let's go to Texas and get rich in the cattle business."

Bill said, "I don't know about the getting rich part, but I'm all for going to Texas." Bill was eighteen years old and had already killed a man. The brutality of the knife fight would serve to somewhat prepare him for the violence of the west.

Chapter 2

The western cowboy borrowed heavily from the South and Central American cowboys who were called "gauchos." Chaps, spurs, western saddles, and horsemanship techniques in cattle handling were learned from the gauchos. The term ranch came from the Spanish *ranchero*. After the Civil War, the price of beef dropped to the extent it was unprofitable to drive them to market. Suddenly, the northern preference for pork changed to beef, and a beef cow worth four or five dollars might be worth as much as forty a head in Missouri or Kansas. Responding to the demand for beef, James G. McCoy established a cattle market in Abilene, Kansas, in 1867.

The famous Chisholm Trail became a major route. The trail was established in 1865 by Jesse Chisholm and ran 600 miles from San Antonio, Texas, to Abilene, Kansas. More a corridor than a trail, the route was as much as fifty miles wide in some stretches. Typically, rivers and Indian lands had to be crossed, but good grazing, relatively level terrain, and higher prices waiting at the destination made the hazards worthwhile.

The extermination of buffalo on the Great Plains opened more grassland for livestock grazing, and the Texas longhorn was the first to fill the void. During the years after the Civil War, hundreds of thousands of wild Longhorn cattle ran free in the valleys, sagebrush areas, and wild land of Texas. They were there for the taking if you had the courage, will, and stamina; but the work was horse and man-killing difficult.

****

Bill and Bud spent the first night on the trail and made a fire, ate some jerked beef, and brewed some Arbuckle. The next day, they arrived in Rosati, Missouri, and checked around to see if they could find a few days' work. Nothing was available. They did luck upon a family who offered their barn and a scoop of oats for the horses and gave them coffee and breakfast before they left headed towards Joplin, Missouri.

The next evening they stopped in Rolla, Missouri, stabled their horses at the livery and got a meal at the Miner's Café (so named by the opening of the Missouri School of Mines and Metallurgy). The school was the first technological learning institution west of the Mississippi River.

While eating at the Miner's Café, an older man walked over to their table and asked if they worked cattle. Embellishing their bona fides at bit, Bill and Bud said they had worked mixed breed Herefords. The man, Bruce Dunner, said he was driving 1,000 head of Longhorn cattle to St. Louis, and one of his drovers got hurt and another quit. He asked if they were looking for work. Bud spoke up and said they would be happy to help with the drive. "What would be our pay?" Mr. Dunner said, "Thirty dollars each and one horse to keep from the remuda."

They agreed to Mr. Dunner's offer and followed him to the camp after finishing their dinner.

Besides Bill and Bud, Mr. Dunner had three drovers and one man who managed the remuda. They were tickled to see two more hands to say the least. They got started at daylight the next morning and bedded the cattle down for the night outside the small town of St. James in Crawford County. Neither Bud nor Bill said anything, but they weren't real excited to be back in Crawford County with the Nuence clan probably out looking for blood. The new guys got the night and owl shifts looking after the cattle, and then after a quick breakfast and coffee, they were back on the trail.

The drovers stopped the herd and let them water from the Meramec River and then bedded them down for the night. Bill and Bud were sitting near the campfire drinking coffee when Mr. Dunner spoke up, "What do you boys have planned when the drive is over?"

Bud replied, "We want to start a cattle ranch."

Mr. Dunner asked, "How much money do you boys have?"

Bud replied, "After you pay us for the drive, we will have a little more than $200.00 between us."

"If I were young and wanted to be in the cattle business, I would go to northeast Texas. There are thousands of unbranded Longhorns roaming prickle pear thickets, sage brush, and hills and hollers for the taking. The problem is, it is gut bustin work, tough on man and horse."

Bud replied, "We had thought about Texas, but Montana is really what we have in mind."

Dunner responded, "Why not go to Texas, build a herd, drive them to Montana and start your ranch." About that time, there was a gunshot from the direction of the herd.

Mr. Dunner and the drovers in the camp jumped on their horses and headed to the herd. When they got there, a man was on the ground leaking a good bit of blood. Mr. Dunner asked the drover, "What happened?"

The drover, Jess Benson said, "Three men were trying to cut the herd. This one got a bit too close, and I put a piece of lead in him. The others tucked tail and ran off."

"A couple of you boys get this rustler back to the camp. If he lives we'll hang him in the morning."

As it turned out the man bled out during the night, and they buried him the next morning. They completed the drive to the railhead in St. Louis without further incident and were paid off by Mr. Dunner, and each man picked a horse from the remuda. Mr. Dunner thanked them for their good work and said, "If I were you I would invest in a pair of chaps. If you go after those Longhorns you will need them. And at least two more horses would be advisable. Horseflesh wears down fast in the work you are fixin to tackle." Dunner gave Bill and Bud a bill of sale for the two horses and wished them well. They thanked Mr. Dunner, went to the River Café, and had supper. Then got a bath and slept in the livery.

Bud and Bill had been on the road for almost a month and were farther away from Texas than the day they left home. Now, they would head west again.

Chapter 3

Bill and Bud traveled from Saint Louis to Joplin, Missouri, with several overnight stops in barns, livery stables, and under the stars. In Joplin, they found a saddle maker who made them chaps. They then went to a blacksmith and ordered a branding iron. After haggling with a livery stable hostler for two days, they finally settled on a price for two half broken mustangs. When they completed the deal on the mustangs, their branding iron was ready: the Slant BB. They left for the Oklahoma Territory the next morning.

When they entered the Indian Territory, they discovered the Cherokee and Osage were occupying the land but didn't seem greatly concerned with the two fellows who were traveling through. When they arrived in South Oklahoma Territory, they were smack dab in the middle of Comanche, Kiowa, and Chickasaw territory. Out in the middle of nowhere, which is modern Jefferson County, they built a pole corral along the side of a hill and built a lean-to with the roof slanted to one side to allow for water drainage. The concept was correct but unneeded because it so seldom rained. They were just North of the Red River and within spitting distance of Texas.

Bill and Bud found feral cattle that had been roaming the sage, cacti, briars, and brambles since the Mexicans were run out of Texas. The feral cattle migrated all over north Texas and southern Oklahoma. In addition to finding cattle without brands, the two cowboys found that the Cherokee,

Chickasaw, Choctaw, Creek, and Seminole Indians were involved in a federal experiment attempting to turn the Five Civilized Tribes into cattle ranchers. The Indians no doubt resented the two cattlemen wannabes encroaching in their areas, but there was no hostility between them and the two young men.

The two cowboys soon found that everything they had been told about the rigors of rounding up feral cattle was true and had been downplayed. It was a horrible experience. Every day produced new thorn scratches on man and horse. The cattle had been wild for years, many of them born in the wild. The longhorn is an ornery critter in the best of circumstances and when they are accustomed to being free, are twice as bad-tempered when they have a rope around their neck.

After two months of eating constant dust, putting salve on thorn scratches on man and horse, saddle sores, and tired backs and butts, the cowboys had sixty-two head of longhorn cattle for their efforts. They had captured more than eighty head of cattle, but some wandered off back to the brush and, although they never saw them, the cowboys were convinced the Indians were stealing some of their cattle. When they brought in a cow that was old and more ill-tempered than most, they turned her into steak meat and jerked beef. Their bacon and beans had long since disappeared.

The two cowboys decided to take a trip across the Red River and see if there were unbranded cows there for the taking. About five miles after they crossed the Red, they saw buzzards circling in the

19

distance. When you saw buzzards circling, they were normally waiting for something to die; if already dead, the scavengers would be on the ground and feasting. Bill looked at Bud and suggested they take a ride over and see what the birds had their eye on. They rode perhaps a half-mile and saw a man staked to the ground and spread-eagled. Both men knew the persons who had done this evil thing might still be in the area. Bud pulled out his field glasses and studied every ridge and flat land in all directions.

Satisfied they were alone; they rode to the man. The man was blistered and swollen from the sun beating down on him for at least a couple days. Bill cut the rawhide thongs which were holding the man down, brought him to a sitting position, wet his bandana, and placed it on the man's lips. Together, the cowboys leaned the man back slightly, and Bill squeezed the bandana and allowed a few drops of water to go into the man's mouth. After repeating this maneuver for a few minutes, the man opened his eyes but couldn't really focus them. They kept giving the man small amounts of water, and after about an hour, he began talking a little and told them his name was Juan Rivera Diaz.

Together, Bill and Bud got Juan on one of their mounts and walked the horses to a small arroyo, built a fire, and put on coffee. After drinking a cup of coffee strong enough to melt granite and eating a few small pieces of jerked beef, Diaz began telling them about his experience with the Comanche. Diaz had been searching for wild horses along the Red and suddenly found himself surrounded by five

Comanche braves. After relieving him of his stallion, weapons, and what little coinage he had, they decided it would be fun to leave him for buzzard bait.

Bill and Bud listened in silence. This wasn't their fight or problem, but without their help, Diaz would die from starvation and the elements. Bud asked Diaz if he knew which direction the Comanche would be headed and was told towards the south where the main tribe was camped. Bill said nothing and just sat and looked off into the evening sky. Bud opined, "Bill, we would have to take Diaz back to Oklahoma Territory to get him a mount, and we have no extra weapons to offer him. He still wouldn't have an outfit."

Bill sat and said nothing for a few minutes and then looked at Diaz and asked, "Juan, what do you know about the Comanche?"

Diaz smiled a weak smile and responded, "Senor, not enough, or I wouldn't have gotten caught with my pants down. We have mostly Apache where I come from. They are bad enough; these savages are far worse."

Bill looked at Bud and said, "If you are game, we can try to catch up with the Comanche and try to get Juan's outfit back." Bud allowed that would be fine. The next morning, they started at daybreak and followed the trail of five unshod ponies and one shod horse. The Comanche made no effort to cover their trail because they, no doubt, thought they were all alone in the world after staking out Diaz. The three men alternated trotting and riding all day long and found a campsite at dark. The fire pit was cold, but the horse droppings were still fairly fresh. They were maybe one day behind the Comanche.

They went through the same routine of taking turns trotting and riding all day long the second day. Just before dusk, Bud saw the five horsemen and the spare horse through his binoculars. The three men stopped, and Bud kept watch with his field glasses. Shortly after dark, they could see the glow from a campfire in the distance. They decided they would wait until early morning and then attempt to sneak up on the camp, get Juan's mount, and then see if they could get his saddle and weapons back.

Around 2 AM, they set out walking the horses, and when they got to within a couple hundred yards of the fire, dismounted and approached on foot. Bill and Bud had their rifles out, and Bud gave Juan his Paterson revolver. When they got near the camp, it was obvious the Indians were sound asleep. Juan turned to Bud and said, "Senor, could I borrow your Bowie?" Juan slipped the Paterson in his waistband and took off his boots and walked as silently as a cat into the camp. He picked the Indian farthest from the fire and clamped his hand over his mouth and slit his throat. He then went to the next Indian and repeated the procedure. Now, there were three live Indians and two armed gringos and one armed Mexican.

Bill and Bud walked into the camp, and each kicked an Indian to wake him. The startled Indians reached for their rifles but immediately realized they were dead if they touched the weapons. They got the three Indians to sit in a group and gathered their weapons. Juan put on his gun belt, put his saddle on the shod pinto, and put his Spencer carbine in its scabbard. Juan turned to Bud and said, "Senor, what do you want to do with these three?"

Bill spoke up and said, "We will take all their cartridges. Leave the two ponies the dead men were riding so they can carry the bodies and let these three go home to their families."

Juan said, "But Senor, they left me for buzzard bait; why not kill them?"

Bud looked at Juan and replied, "These men are no threat to us now. If we kill them for no better purpose than because we can, we are no better than them." With that, they gathered all the cartridge belts, tied the Indians to trees, and took turns napping until first light. When it was light enough to travel, Bill, Bud, and Juan untied the Indians and headed their horses toward the Red.

Juan allowed that he owed Bill and Bud his life and wanted to accompany them back to their camp and help round up feral cattle. Both men agreed they could use his help and promised him a third of any cattle they found for the rest of the adventure.

Chapter 4

Bill, Bud, and Juan made a fine team and worked the brush, briars, and sage and managed to round up sixty more cattle in the first month working together. They decided that they would try to get the cattle to market when they had 200 head. They were motivated by the lack of funds they had on hand. They could eat beef, but without flour and coffee life wasn't much fun.

By the end of May 1859, they had 203 head of Texas longhorn cattle and set out for the port of Galveston, Texas, to sell the small herd and have seed money to start a real cattle business. There was no established trail, but on the other hand, there were no physical impediments to stop them during the 290 mile trail drive. They crossed the Red River into Texas without incident and were making about ten miles a day and had little difficulty.

****

Texas got its name from the Caddoan language of the Hasinai (mostly Pawnee) or *Taysha*, a word which means friends or allies. Alsonso Alvarez de Pineda was the first European to see Texas when he led an expedition sponsored by Jamaica in 1520. Between 1528 and 1535, four survivors of the Alvarez expedition created the first known map of the northern Gulf Coast. They also explored the interior of Texas, traded and at times, were slaves within native groups. Alvarez de Pineda claimed the area that is modern day Texas for Spain.

Spain sent an expedition to establish a mission in East Texas in March 1690. The mission, San Francisco de Los Tejas, was completed near the Hasinai village of Nabedaches in late May and the first Mass was conducted on June 1, 1690.

General Domingo Teran de Los Rios was appointed as the first governor of Texas on January 23, 1691. The Indians who lived near the mission San Francisco had little interest in Christianity but did like the Catholics' cattle and horses and stole them on a regular basis. When the majority of the Spaniards left the mission, they left a smallpox epidemic in their wake. The disease made the Indians more than a little angry, and the remaining Spaniards chose logic over valor and returned to their staging area at Coahuila, Mexico. The Spanish would ignore Texas for the next twenty years.

In 1762, the French gave up their claim to Texas as part of a treaty to end the Seven Years' War. San Antonio became the new provincial capital of Texas. In 1773, settlers returned to East Texas and founded Nacogdoches.

The Spanish and Comanche agreed to a peace treaty in 1785. The Comanche allied with the Spanish to fight the Karankawa and Mescalero and Lipan Apache. The Apache were defeated, and most of the raiding stopped.

In 1799, Spain gave Louisiana back to France. The agreement was signed on October 1, 1800 and went into effect in 1802. In 1803, Napoleon sold Louisiana to the United States. The boundaries of the purchase were ambiguous, and the United States claimed all of Texas. In 1819, the Adams-Onis Treaty was signed, and Spain gave Florida to the United States in exchange for undisputed control of Texas. In 1821, Mexico achieved independence from Spain and took control of Texas.

Spanish control of Texas became Mexican control of Texas. Mexico and Spain shared a common language, and most every river, except the Red River, had a Spanish name. Forty-two of Texas counties and numerous towns and cities have Spanish names. The Spanish introduced European livestock into Texas. Vast herds of cattle grazed on native grasses. The Constitution of Mexico of 1824 joined Texas with Coahuila to form the state of Coahuila y Tejas. The residents of Texas were granted the right to form their own state whenever they were capable. Mexico's General Colonization Law enabled all heads of household, without regard to race or immigration status, to claim Texas land. Part of the logic of the plan was the hope that the new settlers would be able to combat the Comanche.

From the mid-1700s to 1850s, the Comanche were the main native Indian group in the Southwest. The Comanche were a warlike people who stole cattle and horses and killed the Anglos, Mexicans, and other Indians. Their empire collapsed more from smallpox and cholera epidemics than losses in armed conflict. The settlers, Texas Rangers, and the United States Army finished the job.

There was constant bickering between the new Texians and Mexico's government which culminated with the Battle of Gonzalez on October 2, 1835 and launched the Texas revolution. On March 2, 1836, the Texians signed the Texas Declaration of Independence at Washington-on-the-Bravos, which created the Republic of Texas. Skirmishes followed between the Texians and Mexican troops, with the Texians prevailing in each battle. The Mexican congress responded by passing a resolution authorizing the execution of any foreigner found fighting against Mexican forces in Texas.

General Jose de Urrealed took Mexican troops along the coast and executed 300 Texians at Goliad. Mexican President Antonio Lopez de Santa Anna took an army of 6,000 men to San Antonio de Bexar and laid siege to the Alamo Mission. After thirteen days, the Mexican forces overwhelmed the Texians defending the Alamo and killed every man.

On April 21, 1836, the Texian Army led by Sam Houston attacked the Mexican forces in the battle of San Jacinto, captured Santa Anna, and forced him to sign the Treaty of Velasco. On February 28, 1845, the United States Congress passed a bill annexing the Republic of Texas. On December 29, 1845, Texas became the 28th state.

Mexico declared war on the United States on April 5, 1846. All battles were fought in Mexico. Mexico sued for peace on February 2, 1848 and relinquished their claim to Texas.

****

Three days after crossing the Red River, Bill, Bud, and Juan had their first encounter with Indians. A small group of Apache approached them and demanded two of the cattle. The three men discussed the situation and allowed that if they began giving their cattle away, they would all be gone before they got to Galveston. They told the Apache that these cattle were their livelihood, and they would fight to keep them. There were six Apache men and about fifteen women and children.

The leader of the Apache, a tall, impressive man who spoke reasonably good English said, "We are more than the three of you. Do you wish to die?"

Bud looked at the Indian for a couple moments and replied, "You might be able to kill us and steal our cattle and maybe you can't. One thing is for sure; if you try, some of your squaws will be wailing the death chant this day."

The Apache leader looked at the cowboys with complete hatred, and the tension between the two groups mounted until it could almost be cut with a knife. Finally, the Apache leader looked Bud in the eyes and said, "We go. Perhaps we will meet again when we don't have to worry about squaws and children." With that, he wheeled his horse around, and the small group followed him as he rode away.

Bill, Bud, and Juan all expelled a breath of relief. The last thing they wanted was to get into a shooting conflict with anyone, least of all six well-armed Apache. They had no other contact with the

Apache, and even though some were seen at a distance, the Indians never approached the herd. They arrived in Galveston, Texas, on June 27, 1859, and sold 197 head of longhorn cattle to a cattle buyer named John Finnish. After haggling over price for a few minutes, Finnish offered the cowboys $9.00 a head. $1,773.00 in U.S. dollars was a good start on their cattle ranching aspirations. Bill and Bud split the sale of sixty head of cattle two ways and then split the remaining 137 three ways, as was their agreement. Juan now had $411.00 in his pocket, and Bill and Bud had $681.00 each.

Bill and Bud discussed what they should do with the money in their pocket. Bud wanted to deposit $500.00 in the Commerce and Agricultural Bank, which was opened in Galveston in 1847, and was the only chartered bank in Texas. Bill was concerned about putting their money in a bank, largely because of the continuing dispute between free and slave states which he feared would end in war. If a bank failed, their money would be gone. Bud thought it over and decided to follow Bill's advice. Bill's judgement proved sound because the Commerce Agricultural Bank of Galveston, Texas, failed later in 1859, and all the depositors lost their entire savings.

After buying supplies at a local dry goods store and then getting it all stored on a pack horse they had purchased from a hostler for $30.00, which included well-worn panniers, they set out for Oklahoma Territory. They were plumb tired of trying to live out of their saddle bags. They weren't worried about highwaymen because there weren't really any human beings once you got past Houston, Texas, except scattered Indian villages which were a part of the new reservation system.

They arrived back at their camp on July 11, 1859 and got to work rounding up more cattle. They were having to journey farther each day to find feral stock, and the terrain was becoming progressively rougher on them and their horses. They were about ten miles from their camp and had seven head of cattle gathered into a group. They decided to stop, make a pot of coffee, and cook a little bacon and beans. Bill got a small fire started, Bud picketed the horses and took the saddles off them, and Juan was gathering more firewood.

Suddenly, a westerner's worst fears were realized. Juan reached to pick up a couple pieces of wood from a blow down, and without warning, a prairie rattler struck and sunk its fangs into his forearm. Juan screamed but didn't panic and walked to the campfire and sat down. Bud got out his Bowie, slit the site of the bite, and sucked out as much of the blood and venom as he could. Within minutes Juan was having a reaction to the venom or perhaps from the shock of being bitten and was starting to have chills. Within an hour, Juan's arm was warm to the touch, turning red around the area of the bite, and was starting to swell. Bill and Bud knew little about snakebites, but they did know that they needed to keep Juan calm and still and let his body combat the venom.

They wrapped Juan in all the blankets they had, insisted he lay on his side with the arm higher than his heart, kept feeding him water, and hoped he would sweat out the venom. The snake had been relatively small, about three feet long and probably not life threatening, but it sure made Juan sick as a dog for three days. On the evening of the third day, Juan began to feel better, and the chills and fever subsided somewhat. He had a little bacon and beans and said he could ride. Bud told him there was no hurry, and they would leave the next morning if he continued to improve.

The next morning, they began moving the cattle towards their camp. Juan would have a small amount of tissue loss and a scar but no long term effects of the bite. The bite of the Prairie rattlesnake, *Crotalus viridis*, except in the case of a small child or already weakened individual, is rarely fatal. They made frequent stops to allow Juan to rest. He would be fine and have quite a story to tell his grandchildren.

The three friends continued to round up feral cattle and made two more trips from Oklahoma Territory to Galveston, Texas. The next was in October 1859 and the last in February 1860. The two trips garnered them $1,140.00 each based on 380 head of cattle. They divvied up the money between the three of them after sharing expenses and decided they'd had enough of Oklahoma Territory.

Juan was homesick and wanted to go back to Mexico and see his family, and there was a senorita in Piedras Negras who he wanted to see again and maybe marry. Juan said his goodbyes to Bill and Bud and lit out for Mexico. The two cowboys thought on what they wanted to do next. They had enough money between the two of them to buy a small spread and start in the cattle business.

They decided to try to gather feral cattle from the south side of the Red River in Texas and sell them in Galveston. They figured they had gotten everything with horns in the Oklahoma Territory. Unfortunately, circumstances beyond their control ruled their destiny.

They spent considerable time looking for a suitable place to build a ranch, and after finding a site and checking its availability, they decided to put together a herd to sell to have more seed money. They decided to just kinda hunker down for the winter and start rounding up cattle in the early spring of 1861. The cattle were more plentiful in Texas, and when they had put together 120 head of longhorns, they set out for Galveston on April 1, 1861. When they arrived in Galveston on April 20th, the town was abuzz with news of the firing on Fort Sumter and the start of a civil war.

Bill and Bud sold their cattle and were happy to get $6.00 a head in greenbacks. They talked their situation over and decided to go back to Missouri and join the Confederate Army.

Chapter 5

Tensions continued to grow regarding how much control the federal government should exert over the states. Industrialization in the North, restrictions on trade, and certainly slavery had increased tension between the Northern and Southern states. When Abraham Lincoln was elected president in 1860, eleven Southern states seceded from the Union and set up a separate government: the Confederate States of America.

Abraham Lincoln was inaugurated as the 16th President of the United States on March 4, 1861. A little more than one month later on April 12, 1861, the Confederates bombarded Union soldiers at Fort Sumter, South Carolina. This action started a bloody conflict which was to last more than four years and result in the death of about 620,000 human beings from combat, accident, starvation, and disease. More than two million men took up arms for the Union, and almost 1,100,000 joined the Confederate Army. Two of the Confederate soldiers were from the Huzzah Valley in Missouri.

When the Civil War broke out in 1861, both James Budwell Baxter and William Travis Brubaker returned to Missouri to enlist in the Confederate Army. Instead William Quantrill recruited them to fight in his "bushwhackers" known as Quantrill's Raiders. While with Quantrill, they met two brothers who seemed to enjoy killing: Frank and Jesse James. Bill and Bud had no problem with attacking Union supply convoys and patrols. When the goal turned to killing civilians and/or stealing the livestock and food stores of fellow Missourians and leaving them to starve, they decided to leave the raiders and join up with General Nathan Bedford Forrest's cavalry command.

They left Missouri in October 1861 and arrived in Tennessee as Forrest was equipping his battalion. Forrest was an interesting man. Born dirt poor in North Carolina, he became one of the, if not the, wealthiest man in Tennessee through the sale of cotton, land, and slaves. Forrest joined the Confederate Army as a private with the Tennessee Mounted Rifles. As the group increased in number, Forrest used his personal wealth to provide uniforms, weapons, and supplies to support the unit. Forrest was promoted to Lieutenant Colonel and given his own battalion.

Bill and Bud were men of some means but kept their personal finances to themselves because they feared the Confederate government would confiscate their funds if they knew of its existence. Both Bill and Bud had fine horses, their personal Sharps rifles, .36 caliber Paterson's plus two more they had been given when they joined Quantrill. They were welcomed with open arms. Bill was noticed early on as a serious and thoughtful individual with leadership qualities, and Forrest promoted him to Captain within a few weeks of joining his group. Since Bill and Bud had lived alone on the plains, tracked deer and such while living in the Huzzah, and dealt with having to fend for themselves in the elements, Bill was put in charge of scouts. Bud was appointed as his Lieutenant. In all, there were twenty-four enlisted troops under Captain Brubaker's command.

Bill met with his men and briefed them on what he expected from them. All his scouts were backwoodsmen, so he had little in the way of training to convey to them. Bill would keep his scouts in the field with two or three well in front of Forrest's battalion and the same number to both flanks to make sure they weren't surprised by Union forces. After a couple days in the field, the scouts would come in and another group would go out. When Bill was getting to know his troopers, he discovered that one of them was named Ned Nuence and was from the Huzzah. Bill told Ned that he would be glad to have him transferred to another part of the battalion if serving under him was going to be a problem. Ned responded, "What happened between you and Uncle Fid was your own affair. I remember he could be pretty difficult to deal with when he got a snoot full of redeye. I would be honored to be out in the wilds and maybe save the lives of some of these boys. The truth is some of my kin is fighting with the Union and some the Confederacy. I might end up killing kin, or one of them might kill me." With that bit of problem solved, Bill's unit was ready for action.

Bill was sitting by a camp fire drinking a cup of coffee when an older man approached, saluted him, and asked if they could talk for a few minutes. Bill stood and extended his hand and the man, Corporal Bart Strong of Bolivar, Missouri, introduced himself. The thrust of his need to talk to

Captain Brubaker was to seek his help in avoiding Union patrols. Strong explained that he was a sharpshooter and was all by his lonesome when he was out seeking Union officers as targets. As such, it would be mighty helpful if Captain Brubaker would give him briefings on where and the number of patrols he was observing. Going out and getting in an area for an open shot at a Union officer was just part of the problem. Getting back to Forrest's encampment was even more important. The reality was the Union Army didn't take Confederate sharpshooters prisoner. They were executed on the spot.

Bill was impressed with the seriousness with which Corporal Strong took his responsibilities and was even more fascinated when Strong told him that it was his intent to only wound his target and take him out of the field. After the Quantrill experience, it was refreshing to meet a man who had scruples with regard to taking human life. Captain Brubaker and Corporal Strong would meet about twice each week, go over terrain, likely hiding places, and escape routes to get back to their encampment. After a few weeks, Captain Brubaker went to Colonel Forrest and suggested Corporal Strong be assigned to his unit. Strong wasn't a scout, but they were in constant communication, so it would be easier if he was a part of Bill's unit. Colonel Forrest heard Bill out and said it made sense to him and said, "I will have my executive officer make the change. And thanks for bringing this to my attention."

During February 1862, Union General U. S. Grant's army had seized Paducah, Kentucky, and captured Fort Henry on the Tennessee River. Grant's army had surrounded Fort Donaldson and surrender seemed inevitable. Sensing that General Buckner would surrender the fort, Colonel Forrest sent a messenger for Captain Brubaker. When Brubaker reported to Forrest, the Colonel said, "Bill, I fear that General Buckner and the others in command will surrender the fort to Grant. I need for you and your boys to find us a way out of this mess while there is time."

"Yes sir, I will get scouts out immediately and see what we can do."

Later, during the night, the Confederate commanders, General Simon Buckner, General John B. Floyd, General Gideon Pillow, and Colonel Bedford Forrest met to discuss their situation. The three generals had already decided to surrender to General Grant. Forrest looked at the three men and said, "I did not come here for the purpose of surrendering my command." With that, General Buckner gave him permission to try to escape with his battalion.

Forrest stormed out of the meeting and sent for Captain Brubaker. When he arrived, Colonel Forrest asked him, "Bill, have you found us a way out?"

Captain Brubaker responded, "If we are lucky, we might make it."

Forrest and his troops, including Baxter and Brubaker, escaped under the cover of darkness.

Based largely on Brubaker's scouts' ability to keep the 650 men under Forrest's command hidden and undetected by Union troops, they completed a seventy-five mile trek through woods and snow to the relative safety of Nashville, Tennessee.

As is always the case in war, Colonel Forrest, who commanded the battalion, got the credit from the Confederate high command in Richmond, Virginia, for the daring escape, which was fine because it was his decision to make the attempt.

Chapter 6

After their escape from Fort Donaldson, Bill and Bud were bivouacked near Corinth, Mississippi, along with the rest of Colonel Forrest's cavalry battalion. On April 6, 1862, General Albert Sidney Johnston ordered the Confederates to attack Grant's forces which were located at Pittsburg landing on the west bank of the Tennessee River. General Johnson was killed during the engagement and replaced by General P. G. T. Beauregard.

The Confederate army was advancing, but General Beauregard decided to call off the attack and resume the offensive the next morning. Bud and two of the scouts detected General Jon Carlos Buell and his army arriving during the night and informed Colonel Forrest. Forrest went looking for General Beauregard but had no success in finding him. No one knew where the general was. Forrest stumbled upon General William J. Hardee and told him of the second Union army which was approaching. Hardee thought Forrest was just a nervous civilian colonel and told him, "Don't worry, and go to bed."

Hardee's comment infuriated Forrest, and he replied, "If this army does not move immediately, it will be whipped like hell in the morning." General Hardee ignored Forrest's report and comments, and the Confederate army suffered a bloody defeat the following day.

During the engagement Forrest's cavalry, along with a unit of Alabamians, attempted to put a Union artillery battery out of commission. They did manage to place a dent in the battery and killed all the battery horses but were unsuccessful in destroying it. In the face of withering rifle and pistol fire from the soldiers guarding the battery, Forrest was forced to withdraw.

One of the soldiers hit by Union fire was Lieutenant James Budwell Baxter. A rifle ball had hit him in the chest, passed through his left lung, nicked a rib, and lodged in soft tissue in his back. Bill was near Bud when he fell and took him directly to the surgeon. When the surgeon examined Bud, he turned to Captain Brubaker and said, "There is nothing I can do for him."

Bill looked at the surgeon and said, "Put a drain tube in him, and I will find someone to care for him."

The surgeon said, "Captain, I said…" That was all he got out of his mouth before looking down the barrel of a Paterson pistol.

Bill said, "Put the drain in him and bind his chest, and I will find a civilian home to take care of him. The other choice is to join those killed today." The surgeon made the incision, inserted the drain tube into Bud's lung, and had a nurse bind his chest. He then gave Captain Brubaker a couple bottles of Laudanum and said Bud should have a teaspoon of the liquid every few hours if he lived. Bill had a litter made to be drawn behind a horse and had two of his scouts take Bud to Corinth, Mississippi, with instructions to find a home that would care for him. He told the men to tell the people he would come and make financial arrangements for Bud's care in a few days.

When the two scouts, Ira Compton and Ike Cantrell, arrived in Corinth, they went to a house just outside town and knocked on the door. Mrs. Ned Thompson, Sarah, answered the door, and Ira explained their problem. Mrs. Thompson's husband was off fighting with the Confederacy, and she said she would be happy to try to nurse Lieutenant Baxter back to health, but money wasn't necessary. The two scouts reported back to Captain Brubaker and told him what the woman had said and how to locate her home.

Now Sherman was after the Confederates, and it fell to Captain Brubaker to find a way to avoid an open conflict. Forrest had about 350 cavalry troops remaining battle ready, and Sherman had an army. Based on his scouts' reports, Bill selected terrain that was cluttered with fallen logs, brambles, and mud holes in order to slow the advancing infantry. When the Union forces got sufficiently strung out, Forrest attacked them. Forrest wasn't able to do a great deal of damage, but he did harass them enough to allow Beauregard to retire to Corinth in good order.

Bill reported to Colonel Forrest and asked permission to go and check on Lieutenant Baxter. The request was merely perfunctory military courtesy, and Colonel Forrest said, "Yes, by all means go and check on Lieutenant Baxter and give him my compliments."

When Bill arrived at the Thompson home, he was met by Sarah Thompson who greeted him warmly and said that Bud was still alive but gravely ill. His recovery would depend on whether he got a bad infection or pneumonia. The former would make his recovery iffy, and the latter would be certain death. Bill insisted on giving Mrs. Thompson $50.00 in greenbacks to help defray the cost of food and any possible medicines she might need to buy, presuming anything was available. After visiting with Bud for a few minutes and wishing him well, Bill headed back to his unit.

When Bill got back to the bivouac area, he reported to Colonel Forrest and informed him that Bud was still alive, but his recovery was touch and go. Colonel Forrest looked at Captain Brubaker for a couple moments and then said, "Bill, I had a surgeon come to me and say that you threatened to shoot him if he didn't treat Lieutenant Bud Baxter. I told him that he must be taking his own Laudanum. No officer of mine would do such a thing." Colonel Forrest then looked at Bill and said, "I would prefer you not respond to that!"

Captain Brubaker's scouts went back to work making sure the way was clear for the movement of Forrest's cavalry to Chattanooga, Tennessee. Bill had heard nothing from Bud or Mrs. Thompson and was very worried about his friend. On July 23, 1862, Lieutenant Bud Baxter rode up to Colonel Bedford Forrest's command tent and reported for duty. The musket ball would be with Bud his entire life but caused him little discomfort, and his punctured lung had completely healed. When Bud found Bill, he hugged him and thanked him for saving his life when the surgeon refused to treat him.

Bill said, "You would have done the same for me. The only difference is you would have probably shot the surgeon in the knee to remind him to try to save lives." Bill put Lieutenant Baxter back to work. Even though he was still weak, it was the best therapy for him.

Chapter 7

On June 7th and 8th, 1862, General James S. Negley's Union forces attacked the Confederate forces at Chattanooga, Tennessee. General Don Carol Buell began leisurely moving his Army of the Ohio from Corinth, Mississippi, towards Chattanooga to reinforce Negley's troops. The Confederates responded by diverting their reinforcements in the attempt to draw Union troops away from Chattanooga.

Colonel Nathan Bedford Forrest, with his scouts preceding his cavalry units, was dispatched from Chattanooga to retake Murfreesboro, Tennessee. Forrest's troop was joined by two more cavalry units on his way to Murfreesboro, bringing the total of Confederate cavalry to about 1,400. At that time, Murfreesboro, a strategic supply depot on the Nashville and Chattanooga Railroad, was held by a small Union force camped in and around the town.

Colonel Forrest's troops camped at McMinnville on the night of July 12th. Captain Brubaker's scouts captured the Union pickets without firing a shot. After questioning the captured pickets extensively, Bill learned of the uncoordinated Union troop emplacements at Murfreesboro. The Ninth Michigan was camped at Manley's spring. Due to inadequate water and bickering among Union leaders, the other two units were camped at separate locations a mile and one-half northwest of town.

Captain Oliver C. Rounds, Commander of the Ninth Michigan, Company B, and provost marshal of Murfreesboro was holding several local citizens prisoner in the courthouse awaiting execution by order of Union Major General Thomas L. Crittenden. Crittenden had only arrived from Alabama on July 12th and was completely unaware of any Confederate activity in the area.

On the night of July 12th and the early morning hours of July 13th, Captain Brubaker sent out separate units of his scouts. When both groups of scouts reported back that they hadn't engaged any Union forces, Bill reported to Colonel Forrest and gave him the information. On the morning of July 13th, Colonel Forrest celebrated his birthday by approaching Murfreesboro undetected from the east on Woodbury Pike, capturing a Union hospital and a detachment of the Ninth Pennsylvania cavalry detail. Forrest then divided his troops into three groups and attacked the Ninth Michigan at Manley's spring and the Third Minnesota to the west of the Michigan troops.

Colonel Henry R. Lester, commander of the Third Minnesota, refused to come to the aid of the besieged Michigan troops. Colonel William Duffield, commander of the Ninth, held on as long as he could, was wounded, and taken to a field hospital. Lieutenant Colonel John G. Parkhurst relieved Duffield as commander. Colonel Lester's refusal to come to the aid of the Ninth Michigan allowed them to be overrun and forced to surrender. After the surrender, Parkhurst was allowed to march his men through the same Confederate forces several times in order to confuse him and then they were released.

Due to Colonel Forrest's ruse, Lieutenant Colonel Parkhurst reported the Confederate's strength as about three times the actual number. Once he was convinced that the other Union forces had surrendered, Colonel Lester surrendered his troops as well as the attached Kentucky battery. Lester was later court-martialed for cowardice in the face of the enemy.

Colonel Forrest's cavalry captured between 800 and 1,200 Union forces, including Major General Crittenden and Captain Rounds, and set the civilians who were being held for execution free. For his actions in the 1st battle of Murfreesboro, Colonel Forrest was promoted to Brigadier General.

Shortly after receiving the news of his promotion, General Forrest called Captain Brubaker to his headquarters tent and asked him to sit down. Forrest was thoughtful for a few moments and then said, "Bill, you and your scouts have been a great asset to me and kept my butt out of the fire more than once. You deserve to be a Major, but the reality is that I need you so much in your capacity as chief of scouts that I can't afford to remove you. Lieutenant Baxter could no doubt do the job, but the men love you and would charge hell with buckets of water if you asked. I just can't afford to remove you, and if I promote you I must."

Bill smiled at the general and said, "General Forrest, I am perfectly happy with the command I have. The way I view this war, my feeding you information that will help kill the enemy and keep our forces out of harm's way is more important than a gold leaf on my shoulder. I hope my information gathering will help keep more of our troops alive so they can return to their families."

Bill and Bud went on to serve with General Forrest at Hog Mountain in northern Alabama and Chickamauga in southeastern Tennessee. Then they took part in the Mississippi campaigns: Okolona in Chickasaw County, Brice Crossroad near Baldwin, and Harrisburg near Tupelo, in July 1864. Then the campaigns returned to Tennessee; Franklin and then Nashville, in December 1864. The battle at Harrisburg, Mississippi, was arguably the crowning achievement of General Forrest's engagements, but it was also a tragic defeat for the Confederacy.

General Forrest was best known for his cavalry tactics and military instincts. His axiom was "Get there first with the most men." Unfortunately, all his brilliant military achievements were tarnished by his unit's involvement in the Battle of Fort Pillow in April 1864. It seems his troops were overcome by the emotions of the battle and killed some 300 Negro soldiers following the Union's surrender. General Forrest denied to his dying day having ordered the carnage or having knowledge of the incident until it was over. Still, his personal honor and reputation were tarnished by the incident.

General Forrest surrendered his troops at Selma, Alabama, in May 1865. He was paroled and returned to his cotton plantations. During the Reconstruction Period, he received a full pardon from President Andrew Johnson on July 17, 1868. Forrest worked as a planter and railroad president and served as the first grand wizard of the Ku Klux Klan. He later resigned from the Klan and denounced their activities. Nathan Buford Forrest died in 1877 at the age of fifty-six and was buried in Memphis, Tennessee, in what is now the Health Sciences Park.

Bill Brubaker and Bud Baxter had experienced the honor of serving under the command of one of the most capable generals, Confederate or Union, of the Civil War.

The horrible war ended on May 13, 1865, when Confederate General Robert E. Lee surrendered the Confederate army at Appomattox courthouse in Virginia. After four long years of horrible living conditions, constant fear of death or capture, and seeing good men killed or maimed for life, Bill and Bud were free to resume their dream of being cattlemen.

Bud was still bothered some by the musket ball which had gone through his lung and almost killed him, but all in all, he was lucky and physically fit. Bill had survived the conflict without as much as a scratch but would remember the friends he had lost. He knew how lucky he was.

Chapter 8

Once Bill and Bud were mustered out of the Confederate Army they headed out from Corinth, Mississippi, towards Dallas, Texas. It was a rough time in American history and carpetbaggers and scalawags were all over the South. Money was extremely scarce. Confederate money wasn't even good for toilet paper, and very few individuals had greenbacks. Starvation turned once honest men into criminals, and Bill and Bud learned quickly they were to trust no one and keep a sharp eye on their back trail. Bandits were as thick as fleas on a dog's back. Some would as soon kill a man as not.

The word that the Civil War was ending reached the Texas government in April 1865. When the Confederate soldiers heard of the surrender, soldiers in Houston, Galveston, San Antonio, and Austin rioted for their back pay. The Confederacy had no money, and if it did, it would be worthless paper after the war ended. Disgruntled former soldiers attacked government warehouses and stripped them of anything of value. Former soldiers commandeered two trading ships, one from the Far East, and stripped them of their cargo. Some of the seamen fled in fear, others were killed.

On May 13, 1865, the last battle of the Civil War was fought at Palmito Ranch near Brownsville, Texas. A Confederate contingent led by John "Rip" Ford defeated a Union force and killed about 100 troops. After the skirmish, most of the Confederate soldiers got drunk and stayed drunk, others took off for home, and some wanted to fight on and went to Mexico.

After a few days of seeing his forces decimated, Ford released the remaining troops and told them to go home. Ford coined the axiom "Win the battle but lose the war."

Bill and Bud arrived in Dallas, Texas, in July 1865, and saw a town in turmoil. On July 8, 1860, most of Dallas was burned to the ground along with Denton and part of Austin. The arsonists were never discovered. Most people believed it to be Union sympathizers who started the fires. Many of the buildings that were destroyed still hadn't been rebuilt and burned out and decaying structures lined several of the streets in the middle of the town.

The two friends went to the Safford café to have a beef steak, and while they were eating, Bud struck up a conversation with the cook, a man who told them his name was Kaede Higa. Bud always was a curious sort and started asking the man questions. Bud had seen pictures of Orientals, so he knew the man was from somewhere in the Far East, but he had no idea where. The man said he was from Japan and had been on a trading ship that ruffians boarded in Galveston and killed a couple of his shipmates. Believing survival to be the better part of valor, he had jumped off the ship and swam to the dock. After leaving the ship, he had made it to Dallas and was working as a cook. Bud asked Higa what the name Kaede meant in Japanese, and the man said, "Maple leaf. And before you ask, half the people in Japan are named Higa. Kinda like Jones or Smith here in America."

Bud kept talking and finally asked Higa if he could ride a horse. Not real good was the response. He had ridden some in Japan, but it had been years. After yacking back and forth for the better part of an hour while Higa was cooking, Bud looked at Bill and said, "We sure could use a cook and someone to help with the work."

Bill thought for a couple minutes and then replied, "Its fine with me. You work it out with him if you can, but he will have to pull his weight." Bud discussed their plans with Higa, and he allowed working with them would be more interesting than cooking in the Safford café and joined up with them.

The following day when the three men were getting their horses saddled to leave, a large, mean-looking man started in on Higa calling him a Chink and threatening to whip him. Bill and Bud just kinda stood aside and watched to see what was going to happen next. Higa looked at the man and said, "I am Japanese, not Chinese, and you should go about your business."

The man lunged at Higa who sidestepped, grabbed the man's arm, and flipped him to the ground with a hip roll. The man got up, smiled, lunged again and was met with a sidekick in the right knee which sent the big man to the ground. Higa looked at the man, who was in obvious pain, and said, "You need to go about your business before you get hurt." The man pulled a Bowie knife as he got up and lunged at Higa. Kaede side-stepped and brought his knee up against the man's knife arm and bought his elbow down at the same instant. Bill and Bud heard the man's arm snap like a dead branch.

The man began pawing at his gun with his good arm and Bill pulled his Paterson and said, "Right now you got a sore knee and broken arm. If you get that hog leg out of the holster, you will die here in the street."

The man bristled but didn't try to draw the pistol. Bill told Higa to get the man's gun and throw it in the watering trough. Kaede quickly complied, and the three mounted up and started down the street. Bud looked at Bill and said, "I have always been good at picking men who were capable. That's why I hang around with you. You're capable." Bill just shook his head and said nothing at all.

After they had ridden for a couple miles Bill looked at Kaede and asked, "How did you learn to fight like that? You made whipping that giant seem like child's play."

Kaede smiled and replied, "I'm not sure it has an English name. We are taught as children to defend ourselves by using a system of unarmed combat that was developed hundreds of years ago. Basically, it is the art of using the other person's size and strength against him. The Japanese term is *bujutsu*, and it is the art of combat without weapons. I was born into a family of status and wealth, and they sent me to a school to learn these skills."

Bud looked at Kaede and said, "Well, whatever it's called, I want you on my side if we get in a scrape."

Bill and Bud had close to $2,000 between the two of them after buying tools and a rifle for Kaede which would be seed money to purchase a tract of land for their ranch. They were headed for Hopkins County, Texas, and their goal was to put together 1,000 head of stray longhorn cattle. They would take the herd to market and leave the best 100 or so bulls and heifers they had found to use for breeding stock to get their ranch started.

Before leaving Dallas, Bill posted a letter to his father telling him that he and Bud would be in Hopkins County, Texas, and they were ready for the Hereford bull and heifer. He asked him to please telegraph them at Sulphur Springs, Texas, when the cows were shipped from Saint Louis, Missouri, and they would go to Dallas and pick them up.

Chapter 9

Hopkins County, Texas, contained 100 natural springs and sweet grass land. The only towns of any size were Sulphur Springs, about eighty miles southwest of Dallas, and Mount Pleasant, which was more than 100 miles from Dallas. Hopkins County was created from parts of Lamar and Nacogdoches counties in March 1846, by the first Texas state legislature.

The land was filled with deer, turkey, and a few cougars. Sulphur Bottom was a tangle of trees and brush which contained hundreds of Texas longhorn cattle that had wandered in from Mexican herds and Texas cattle left unattended during the Civil War. The Blackland Prairie consisted primarily of deep, loamy, moderately well-drained soil. White Oak Creek was a couple miles north of where the Slant BB cabin was planned to be located and ran east and west. A smaller creek fed off it and was about 200 yards in front of the selected cabin site and ran south. The ranch house, corrals, and outbuildings, once constructed, would be well above the creek elevation, so flooding wouldn't be a threat. This site would give the cowboys a view of the valley to the left and right for more than a mile and a little more than two hundred yards to the copse of Cyprus and Pine trees which lined the far side of the creek. Bill and Bud selected this location to start their ranch. They decided to first build a corral for their mounts and then a tack shed to store their saddles and tools before starting on the cabin. They had stopped in

Sulphur Springs, talked to the telegraph operator and told him they were expecting a telegraph message and would pay whoever delivered it to them $2.00 in greenbacks.

Once they got the corral built and the storage shed finished, they turned their attention to the construction of a log cabin. There were plenty of trees in Sulphur Bottom, so they set about cutting and dragging logs to construct the dwelling. After the exterior walls were formed by notching logs and laying them in a crisscross fashion, they left two window openings and a door opening, and began the process of chinking between the log openings with sod and grass. They then used pine lodge poles as rafters for the roof and sealed the gaps with sod chinking. They mixed soil and sand to make dabbing to cover the chinking on the exterior vertical walls. They cut sod into blocks and built a fireplace and flue for cooking and heat in the winter. Bud was right handy with wood tools, and he had bought the essentials in Dallas while they were there: a hand saw, crosscut saw, hand shave, and plane. He had also picked up hinges for the door and windows, made two windows and a door with rifle ports for all three, and made locking bars for the windows. There was a blind spot on the rear of the cabin, but by the structure being built with the back against the hill, it was inaccessible unless a hostile wanted to drop about thirty feet to the roof. They had built a sod berm to divert the water runoff from the hill. Then they dug a flume on each end of the berm at the back of the cabin.

Bud made all the rustic furniture including a table, and benches, and used an awl to drill holes for pegs for hanging hats, coats, gun belts, rifles, and other items. It took a week to build the log house, and as Bill and Kaede were doing the chinking and dabbing, Bud started on the furniture which was a more tedious and time consuming task. Finally, after a month, the log cabin was finished, not a thing of beauty, but functional and water tight.

About the same time the structure was completed, a young man arrived with a telegraph message. The bull and heifer should be in Dallas by the time Bill got there. Bill paid him the $2.00 and left the next morning for Dallas. It took two days to get to Dallas. The bull and heifer were there in a small holding pen next to the stockyards. Bill put leads on both the bull and heifer and set out for Hopkins County. Five days later the Slant BB was ready to get into the cattle breeding business.

It was 1866, and Bill, Bud, and Kaede were completely isolated from civilization and surrounded by different tribes of Indians, some friendly and some not. Bill and Bud were well armed with Spencer rifles and three Paterson pistols each. They had bought Kaede a lever action Henry rifle in .44 caliber rim fire, and Bud gave him one of his Paterson revolvers. They were relieved and pleased to learn that Kaede could shoot as well as he could fight.

The Comanche traveled from North to South and returned along a trail which crossed near Big Springs, Texas, which was about 450 miles south by southwest from Hopkins County. But the Comanche tended to wander, and the Apache were always a concern. Three men, no matter how well armed, were always at risk from Indian attack. The three men had been warned while in Dallas that Strong Bear and his Comanche warriors were causing mischief along the frontier, and a few settlers had been attacked and killed. They were as ready as they could get.

Strong Bear had given his permission for One Eye and a contingent of about twenty braves to head south into Texas to raid settlements. Fortunately, the raiding party was very accommodating and waited until the cowboys had their cabin completed before they arrived to steal the Slant BB horses and try to burn down the dwelling. Actually, they just arrived when they arrived and probably didn't even know the men had taken up residence, or perhaps, the Comanche had never even been in the location and merely stumbled on the three men.

Luckily, the men were sitting outside the door of the cabin drinking an early morning Arbuckle when the Comanche came screaming and storming out of the copse of trees and crossed the creek. It was all asses and elbows as the three men all tried to get in the door at the same time to get their rifles. Bill got in the door first and grabbed his Spencer and cut down the Indian that was in the lead of the pack. Seconds thereafter, Bud and Kaede were out the door and taking aim on the charging Comanche. Both men fired at precisely the same time, and two more braves hit the ground. The Indians wheeled their horses around and lit out for the copse of trees. The men didn't shoot as the hostiles fled. No reason to kill if you don't have to.

Kaede looked at Bill and said, "Will they come back?"

Bill didn't reply immediately, pondered the question, and responded, "Hard to say. They have three dead friends, and they won't like that. We have nine excellent saddle horses and a pack horse. Horses are wealth to the Comanche. They will want them mighty bad. But we are situated well, and they can't get to the corral without being in the open and have seen what our rifles can do. The element of surprise is over, I think they will leave."

Bill guessed wrong! The day passed without incident, no noise from beyond the creek, no movement, and no reason to believe the Comanche were still around. Neither Bill nor Bud was well versed on Indian warfare or habits. They had been told that Indians won't attack at night because they believed their spirit would wander in darkness if they were killed at night. Wrong again!

The cowboys stayed in the cabin and took turns napping and watching from the windows and door slot. They had food and water, so they could wait out the Indians if they had too. The horses would like some grain but that would have to wait.

The bull and heifer were in a short run next to the corral and more important than the horses. A couple hours after dark, Bud slipped out of the cabin and used the moonless night to hide his movements as he went to the side of the corral nearest the cabin and lay down. Kaede looked at Bill and said, "I know nothing of Indians, but I know how to sneak up on people. That was part of my training as a child. I will take a knife and see if I can find out if the Indians are still around if you want." Bill just nodded his agreement.

A little after midnight Kaede slipped out of the darkened cabin and circled to the left towards the creek. When he got to the creek, he crossed upstream from where the Indians had crossed and got on his belly and started moving towards the copse of trees. After about an hour of wriggling along on his stomach, he heard the faint murmuring of voices in a language he couldn't understand. Having found out what he needed to know, he started back to the creek and after a few yards, came face to face with an Indian who was headed towards the Comanche camp. They startled each other, and each pulled out their knives. The Indian lunged at Kaede. Kaede sidestepped and drove his blade into the side of the Indian and pinned him to the ground with his knee on the hostile's knife arm, left hand over the Comanche's mouth, and held him down with his body weight until the Comanche stopped thrashing. He then got up and went back to the cabin and told Bill of his discovery and the short knife fight.

Three Indians were dead from the initial attack and one from the knife fight with Kaede which left fifteen or sixteen still alive and well. Around 2 AM, three Indians came across the creek and headed towards the corral. When they got close to the pole gate, Bud fired his Paterson and hit one of the Indians in the chest area. One of the two remaining braves rushed him with a tomahawk ready for action, and Bud shot him in the stomach. The third brave lit tail for the creek and protection of the trees.

Five Comanche were now dead, and one badly wounded leaving around ten still able to cause mischief. Bud decided the threat to the horses was over, so he got up and headed towards the cabin. After about ten feet, he felt a terrible sting in his left upper leg and saw an arrow shaft sticking out. He had no idea of where the shooter was but ran and hopped to the cabin door and got inside.

Kaede had gotten a little medical training while aboard ship, so he took charge of treating Bud's wound. There was no way to pull the arrow back out through the entrance site, so Kaede cut the shaft off a few inches from the leg. He then probed around on the other side of Bud's leg until he found a hard spot indicating the site of the arrowhead. Kaede went to the fireplace and got a small piece of kindling and told Bud to bite down on it to spare his teeth. There was a jug of whiskey on a shelf, and Kaede got it, bathed his knife, took a big swig, and offered a snort to Bud who declined. Working as fast as he could, Kaede made an incision and then pushed the arrow through the leg and out the incision site. He then grabbed the arrowhead and jerked the arrow free.

Kaede then applied a generous amount of whiskey to the entrance and exit sites of the arrow and bound the wound with a clean cloth. There was no damage to anything but fat. If the Indian hadn't put poison or feces on the arrowhead, Bud should be fine.

Shortly after sunrise, a lone Comanche rode across the creek and advanced towards the cabin with his hands up. When he got to within about thirty feet of the cabin, Bill went out the door to talk with him. The Comanche looked at Bill and said, "I am One Eye. You and your friends are great warriors. You only kill when you must. We will leave you in peace."

Bill said nothing for a couple moments and then replied, "I am called Brubaker. Where did you learn to speak the white man's language?"

One Eye responded, "We captured a young white child who I adopted. She taught me your tongue."

Bill nodded and replied, "You have a wounded man by the corral. We will attend to him as best we can. Leave one horse; if he lives, we will allow him to ride out when he recovers. When we round up longhorns, you are welcome to stop and take one or two to feed your people as you pass through our ranch. Leave the two short horn cows alone. We wish to be your friends."

One Eye said, "It is well. You have my word we will not fight you again. If Small Eagle lives, his family will remember your kindness. We go now and take our dead." With that, One Eye turned his horse and rode back across the creek and into the trees.

Bill and Bud were amazed that the Indians could lose friends and family and still respect and honor those who had killed them. Kaede said the

Indians were much like the Japanese warriors, the Samurai, and their code called *Bushido* which had seven elements: rectitude, courage, benevolence, politeness, veracity, loyalty, and honor.

Chapter 10

After assuring themselves that One Eye and his warriors had departed, Bill and Kaede went to the corral and got Small Eagle. The Indian was small of stature, and they had no difficulty in carrying him to the cabin and laying him on the floor. Bill went back and put the Comanche pony in the corral with the other horses and got all the mounts some oats from the tack shed. Kaede started working on Small Eagle's wound. The bullet had entered to the right of the intestinal mass and apparently hadn't hit any vital organs, but it did make a large exit hole. The Indian had lost a lot of blood, and Kaede wasn't sure at all that he would be able to save him. Kaede poured some Rye whiskey on both the entry and exit sites of the bullet and then put some Holloway's ointment on the wounds. Holloway's contained aloe, myrrh, and saffron and would hopefully aid in the healing process.

Small Eagle was conscious and didn't seem to fear the three white men, or if he did, he hid his feelings well. Kaede gave the Indian some water to drink and then skimmed some broth from stew that had been heated during the day and put it in a bowl. Kaede spooned the broth to the Comanche lad, and it appeared that the nourishment had a desirable effect and perked the young Indian up a mite.

The day after One Eye and his warriors rode off, a new group of Indians showed up at the spread. This time, it was an Apache named *Taklishim*, which meant Gray One in English, and six of his followers.

The thrust of Gray One's visit was to get Small Eagle so that they could no doubt skin him alive or stake him out for the buzzards to feast on. The Apache and Comanche were mortal enemies, and Gray One had encountered the tracks of One Eye's Comanche party shortly after they left the spread. He followed their back trail to the ranch, and when he saw the Comanche pony in the corral, he knew he had hit pay dirt.

Bill came out of the cabin with rifle in hand and said, "I am called Bill Brubaker. What can I do for you?"

Gray One looked at Bill like he was crazy and said, "I am called Gray One. We want the Comanche you have in your cabin. Give him to us, and we go in peace."

Bill looked at the Indian for a couple moments and replied, "We have no quarrel with the Apache. You are welcome to come when you are hungry and kill a longhorn beef to feed your people, but this thing you ask I cannot do."

Gray One was angry and threatening, "You are friend of the Comanche? The Comanche are our enemies."

"We wish to live in peace with all who live in this land. If an Apache brave was injured and in our cabin, we would not give him to the Comanche. This Comanche is in my care and under my protection."

Gray One looked at Bill for a few moments and said, "You are honorable man. This Comanche cannot stay with you forever. When he leaves, we kill him."

Bill looked at Gray One and said, "When the Comanche is well enough to ride we will escort him to the edge of our land. What happens then is between the Apache and Comanche. That is my word on the matter."

Gray One said, "So shall it be."

Bill, Bud, and Kaede had been on the spread for almost a month and hadn't rounded up one cow. In fact, they hadn't even looked for cows, and it looked like it was going to be a couple more weeks before Small Eagle would be able to travel, and they could start rounding up feral cows. Bud was recovering well from being shot in the leg with the arrow, and while he still had a limp, he could ride and work. Within a week, Small Eagle was up and moving around. Communication was a problem because the Indian spoke no English and none of the three cowboys spoke any Comanche. They had managed to relate each other's names, and Small Eagle was learning a few English words. Hungry seemed to be the one word he understood best.

As the days passed, Small Eagle learned more and more English words and got to the point that he could communicate in very limited vocabulary. Basically, the Indian spoke in one, two, or three word sentences, but he could get the idea across. The Indian seemed content being with the three men and seemed to enjoy their chit-chat, joking, and ribbing back and forth and often laughed out loud at their antics.

After a week, Kaede figured Small Eagle was able to travel and told Bill it was time to let him get started back to his tribe. Bill sat down with Small Eagle and with gestures and words told him it was time for him to leave and that the next night they would take him to the edge of their land, and then he would be on his own. The Indian smiled and thanked them for their help and kindness.

Around midnight the next night, Bill, Bud, and the Comanche started out under cover of darkness towards the north. After about an hour of walking their horses, Bill figured they were at the edge of their land. He shook hands with Small Eagle, as did Bud, and bid him well.

Small Eagle was completely out of sight in a matter of seconds. Bill and Bud had no way of knowing if the Indian made it back to his people or if the Apache captured him, but they had kept their word to One Eye. Actually, they had done more than kept their word because they had protected the Comanche brave from the Apache.

The cowboys turned their horses to the south and headed back to the cabin. It was time to round up some cows and get on with their plans.

Chapter 11

The following morning the cowboys were up early, placed the panniers on the pack horse, and packed them with coffee, beans, and bacon, and a couple broadaxes to fall trees to make a corral for their remuda. They then got their individual string of horses and headed out to the brush and briars to round up wild longhorn cattle. There wasn't really anything they could do to secure the cabin or shed; if Indians came by and decided to burn everything, they certainly could. The Comanche were in their debt, even though they had killed five of their braves. The Apache would not bother their cabin because they had kept their word to Gray One, and a man's word was sacred to the Apache. They couldn't leave the Herefords penned up and didn't want to leave them to roam, so they took them along.

There was a concern regarding the outlaws roaming this area of Texas. Benjamin Bickerstaff, Bud Lee, Josiah Thompson, and other outlaws were committing murders and robberies with impunity all over northeastern Texas. So far, Bill, Bud, and Kaede had yet to cross paths with any of the outlaw bunch, but on the other hand, the cowboys were well armed and weren't easy pickins. Low risk was what appealed to outlaws. In was September 1866, and two companies of the Sixth Cavalry under command of Captain Adna R. Chafee were chasing the outlaws all over northeast Texas but having little success in finding them and bringing them to justice.

The longhorns in northeast Texas had been running wild since the start of the Civil War and were deep in the evergreen shrub bogs, cypress swamps, and pines overgrown with briars and brambles. When the cowboys reached a place where they saw cattle droppings and lots of tracks, they stopped and set up shop. Their first order of business was to drop a few smaller pine trees over which to erect and stretch canvas to protect them somewhat from the elements. Then they built a pole corral to house their remuda and hold the Herefords.

The next morning they began the process of trying to drive the wild longhorns out of the bogs and briars. By mid-afternoon, they had managed to get ten cows out and around the camp site. Bill had lassoed an old brindle bull and led him to the camp and staked him out. The cows stayed around the bull, and the stage was set to add to the herd. Every couple days, Bill would move the old bull so that he had plenty of grass, and every day, the cowboys added to their herd by a few head of cattle. After the first week they had fifty head of cattle.

On the eleventh day of the roundup, Bud was riding in one of the Cyprus swamps and came upon a small lean-to shelter. He got down off his horse and walked over to the lean-to and took a look around. He discovered someone was living there. There were coals from a fire that were still warm and some pieces of ragged clothing. Bud looked around but saw no human, only evidence of human occupancy. As he mounted his horse, he saw movement out of his peripheral vision and looked in the direction of the movement. What he saw startled him, a filthy young white girl dressed in rags was standing partly behind a tree and looking at him. Bud dismounted and walked slowly towards the girl who started to run. Bud called out, "Hey, don't run. I'm not going to hurt you." The girl stopped and looked at Bud but made no movement to come closer or run away. Bud turned and walked back to the crude shack and sat on his haunches and waited.

In a few minutes the girl walked up very tentatively, apprehensively, and obviously fearful. Bud smiled and said, "What's your name, girl?"

The girl meekly said, "I am called White Bird."

Bud shook his head in bewilderment and asked, "Do you have a Christian name?"

White Bird answered, "Betty Wilson. I was called Betty Wilson."

Bud went on to ask White Bird, aka Betty Wilson, why she was all alone in the middle of a swamp. Betty explained that she was with her parents in a small wagon train and had been sent to a creek to get water. While she was at the creek, Indians attacked the wagon train and killed everyone. She stayed hidden by the creek and waited until the Indians left and then went to her parents. Her father was scalped, and mother hacked to death. She gathered a few possessions and headed out on foot. After a couple days, she was discovered by a small group of Cherokee Indians, and they took her in and named her White Bird. She stayed with the Cherokee for about two years. Then the Comanche attacked the

69

little group, and she managed to escape in the confusion and fighting. That was about a month past, and she had been alone in the swamp eating anything she could find and sleeping in the little lean-to she had built from dead limbs and vines.

Bud didn't know what to do with Betty, but he sure wasn't going to let her stay out in the middle of a bog by herself. He mounted his horse, reached down and swung the girl up and behind the saddle, and rode back to the camp. When he arrived, he dismounted, helped the girl down, got her a bar of soap, and said, "There is the creek. Go and get yourself cleaned up, and I will see if I can find some clean clothes for you."

Bud took the liberty of taking some of Kaede's extra clothes which were large on Betty but better than the rags she had on when Bud found her. They would have to take her to Dallas when they moved the cattle back to the spread, but for now, she would have to stay with them. Bill and Kaede came back right before sundown with three cows and were amazed at the sight of the girl. Bud had some beef stew on and ready to eat, and they sat down to supper. Betty ate like she had never seen food before. They made the girl a pallet near the fireplace, and she immediately fell asleep.

After being sure the girl was asleep, Bill and Bud discussed what they were to do with her. She was probably twelve to fourteen years old but small for her age. They agreed it would be best to take her to Dallas and see about placing her with a family or perhaps an orphanage. With that decided, they settled in for the night.

The girl would have to stay with them for about a month because their goal was to gather at least 100 head of cattle, and they were still about forty head short. They soon discovered that the girl was a worker and could cook. She started cleaning the cabin and taking pans and cups to the creek to wash. Then she mixed some meat in the cookpot with some wild onions she had dug near the cabin and added some water and salt. Bud watched in amazement and smiled at Bill.

Since they would be leaving the girl alone at the cabin while they were rounding up cattle, Bill thought it best that she know how to shoot a rifle. They had two Sharps .52 carbines which they had brought along as spare weapons. Bill took Betty out beside the cabin and sat some rocks up against the hill and backed off about thirty yards and showed Betty how to aim and squeeze the trigger. Bill handed her the carbine and a couple extra cartridges and told her to try to hit one of the rocks.

Betty took aim, fired, ejected the spent cartridge, put another in the chamber and fired again hitting the next rock. She looked at Bill with a wry smile and said, "Nice rifle. My daddy taught me to shoot when I was just a little girl in Arkansas."

Bill just shook his head and said, "Well, you sure showed me on that one. I think you will be fine. Just make sure at whom you are shooting."

Reasonably comfortable with leaving the girl alone, the three cowboys left the Herefords in Betty's care and headed out the next morning to round up more cattle.

Chapter 12

Bill, Bud, and Kaede returned after two days of backbreaking work in the bogs and briars and had thirteen cattle for their combined efforts. This brought their total herd to seventy-three, presuming none had wandered back to the bogs. When they got their saddles off the horses, rubbed them down, and gave them each a scoop of grain, they headed for the cabin. When they entered the cabin, they were amazed. There was a bouquet of wild flowers on the table, a pot of Arbuckle hanging on the fireplace, a pot of chili made, and three plates and cups sitting on the dust free table. The aroma of the chili filled the cabin, but even without the smell of food, the cabin just smelled different. Bill asked Betty what was different, and she responded, "I aired out the cabin, swept out a few pounds of dust and dirt, and let sunlight come in the door and windows to clean the air of horses and stinky cowboys." The reality was Betty had turned a dreary ramshackle cabin into a home for the group.

The three cowboys were exceedingly pleased with what Betty had done with the cabin, and though she was a good cook, there was the problem of her being out in the wilds with three grown men. The cowboys sat Betty down with the intent to tell her they would be taking her to Dallas for placement with a caring family. Apparently, Betty had thought about what they planned to do and was ahead of them, which was normally the case.

Bill was the spokesman for the cowboys and looked at Betty and said, "Betty, we need to take you to Dallas and find a decent home for you."

Betty looked at each of the men in turn and replied, "You three are my family. I don't want to go to Dallas, and I don't want to live with anyone else."

Bill said, "We understand. We think of you as a part of our group, but it isn't proper for a young girl to be bunking with three grown men."

Betty was ahead of him again and responded, "I've been thinking on that. This little cabin is crowded. Why not build another cabin but smaller, put in a connecting room to join both cabins, buy a wood stove, and use the connecting room for cooking and eating. I can live in the new cabin, and the three of you can have this cabin all to yourselves. But I wouldn't be at all upset if one of you would take me to Dallas and buy me some decent clothes and shoes that fit."

The three cowboys looked at each other and just shook their heads. Bill looked at Bud and said, "Looks like you need to get your tools out and get on this construction project. I will leave tomorrow morning with Betty, get her some clothes, and buy the supplies we need. Kaede, if you will, check all the horses and pay special attention to their hooves. Bill looked at Betty and said, "Betty, if anyone asks, you're my sister."

The following morning Bill saddled two horses, put the panniers on the pack horse, and he and Betty set out for Dallas. As they were about to leave Bill turned to Bud and Kaede and said, "We will be gone for about a week; try not to poison yourselves with your own cooking." He then laughed at his joke and started southwest towards Dallas. Bill and Betty put their horses into a slow trot, made good time, and arrived at the little town of Emery, Texas, during the late afternoon. They went into the Emery Café for a meal of chili beans, coffee, and a piece of apple pie. The dry goods store was closed so Bill found a family, John and Margaret Jackson, to take Betty in for the night. He then went to the livery stable, attended to the three horses, got them a scoop of oats, and bedded down for the night.

The following morning Bill went by the Jackson home, picked up Betty, and thanked them for taking her in for the night. They allowed it was their pleasure. They then went to the dry goods store and were able to fill their supply list and find suitable dungarees, shirts, and boots for Betty. The store didn't have a cook stove, but Bill would get one ordered from Mount Pleasant. Since they had everything they needed, they mutually agreed there was no reason to ride on to Dallas. Betty rolled up Kaede's clothes and put them behind her saddle, and they headed back to the spread.

About five miles northeast of Emery, they were confronted by two rough looking men who blocked their path. The men were wearing torn and well-worn clothes, were filthy, and had tobacco stains on their beards. Bill pulled up and looked the men over and asked them what they wanted. The larger of the two men replied, "Fine looking pack you got on that horse. There must be a month's supplies in them panniers."

Bill immediately knew that he was in trouble and told Betty to move her horse to the side so that she would be out of the line of fire if shooting started. She backed her horse up a few paces and to the right side of Bill. The man looked at Betty and said, "You are a fine looking girl. I'll wager you haven't been deflowered. I can take care of that for you."

Betty just looked at the man and cocked the Sharps that was lying across her saddle pommel and said, "I don't think so."

Bill looked at both men and said, "You two would do well to ride on and leave us alone. We don't want any trouble." For the first time in his adult life, Bill was scared. He knew that he was proficient with a pistol, had practiced drawing and firing the weapon, but he didn't know how good he was compared to other men who lived by the gun. Bill had killed men during the war and defended himself against Indians, but he had never stared into the eyes of a man who meant to kill him. Like the knife fight when he was still a teenager, it was to be a day of reckoning.

The large man said, "Friend, you got troubles whether you want them or not." And with that, he went for his pistol. Without the slightest hesitation, Bill pulled his Colt 1860 and put a .44 caliber slug in the man's chest, and the man fell off his horse. Bill immediately recocked the pistol and the other man threw up his hands and said, "Don't shoot me, Mister, please don't shoot me."

Bill had the revolver pointed at the second man's chest and said, "Take that shooter out by the handle with your left hand and drop it on the ground, then take that rifle out of the scabbard and drop it, then get off the horse on my side so I can see you, and then lie down on your stomach."

The man on the ground looked at Bill and in a wheezing voice said, "You shot me you bastard."

Bill looked at the man and said, "I suspect that is what you had in mind for me. I told you to ride on." Bill got down off his horse and told Betty to keep the Sharps pointed at the smaller man who was lying on his belly. He walked over to the man he had shot and examined his wound and saw he had been hit in his right lung. The man was having trouble breathing and was coughing up frothy bright red blood which indicated that an artery had been severed. Bill relieved the man of his pistol, took the cylinder out, threw away the shells, and then walked over to the other pistol which was lying on the ground and repeated the process of removing the bullets. Both men were carrying Spencer rifles, so Bill ejected the shells from each and put the cartridges in his saddle bags.

Satisfied that the men were no longer a threat, Bill told the smaller man to get up and try to get the injured man on his horse. Perhaps he would live and perhaps not. Bill told the smaller man to take the wounded man to Emery and see if there was a sawbones in the town.

The smaller man said, "I can't do that. We are both wanted and would be shot on sight. I will make a camp and see if he lives or dies. His name is Bud Weller, and mine is Fred Simpson. I appreciate you not killing me." Bud Weller died while Simpson was talking to Bill.

Bill looked at Simpson and said, "I don't think Weller will need that Spencer, and Betty could use a repeater. We'll take it with us. You will have to take care of his body. He was your friend."

Bill and Betty started their horses back up the trail towards the northeast. Bill didn't get any pleasure from shooting another human being, but the man hadn't given him any choice. The men would have killed him, raped Betty, and then killed her if Bill hadn't been more proficient with his pistol than Weller. If nothing else came from the encounter, Bill was assured that he was competent with his sidearm and found his Colt 1860 much more reliable than his old Paterson.

When they arrived back at the cabin, Bud had already converted the window area on the east side of the cabin into a doorway and was in the process of building a room which was to be about ten feet by ten feet for the kitchen and eating area. After two weeks, the eating area and the small cabin for Betty were completed, and Bud went about the task of making her a bed, chair, small table, and pegs on which she could hang her hat and clothes and Spencer rifle.

The small cabin for Betty seemed a solution to any hint of impropriety between the men and the girl. Bill rode to Mount Pleasant and ordered a Charter Oak stove made by the Excelsior Stove Works, Saint Louis, Missouri. Delivery was promised within a month, six weeks at the outside. Now the cowboys could get back to the job of rounding up longhorn cattle.

Chapter 13

Bill, Bud, and Kaede renewed their cattle gathering work. They would come back every couple of days to bring cows and check on Betty. On one of their returns to the cabin, they discovered the Charter Oak stove had been delivered and the piping installed. Betty had played with the stove and had perfected the baking of biscuits. She tested her skill on the cowboys with some hot biscuits and sorghum. She thought she was going to have to get her rifle to get them out of the kitchen.

Over the next few months Bill, Bud, and Kaede rounded up about 150 head of longhorns, bringing their total herd to about 200 head of cattle, far less than the 1,000 they had hoped to find. At that point, they needed to get the cattle to a market and secure additional funds to start a cross-breeding cattle operation.

It was the spring of 1867, and Bill, Bud, and Kaede realized they needed to join their small herd with a larger drive to the market in Fort Sumner, New Mexico. The cowboys had heard that John Chisum was going to make a large cattle drive, and Bill suggested he ride to the Chisum ranch in Denton County to see if the cattle baron would allow them to mix their cattle with the herd going to Fort Sumner.

John Chisum and Jesse Chisholm were not related. Jesse Chisholm was never in the cattle business and developed the Chisholm Trail which was actually a wagon trail from Fort Leavenworth, Kansas, to Council Grove, Oklahoma, that was used to deliver goods to Chisholm's several trading posts along that route. John Chisum was a cattle baron and developed the Chisum Trail which was used for cattle drives from Texas to Fort Sumner and Santa Fe, New Mexico.

Bill left on the 10th of March 1867 and got to the Chisum spread on the evening of the 12th where the cattle baron warmly greeted him. Bill had dinner with Mr. Chisum and was told that he was welcome to join his small herd with the cattle which would be driven to market. Chisum looked at Bill and said, "Can you get your herd here by the 3rd of April? We will leave on the morning of the 5th, and your cattle will have to be segregated from the main herd until we get them tallied and trail branded for the drive."

Bill looked at Chisum and replied, "We will be here. I have two men and a female cook. Do you have any problem with them coming along?"

Chisum scratched his chin, thought a couple moments, and replied, "Your partners are certainly welcome, but a woman on a trail drive presents all kinds of problems. I don't think I can allow that."

Bill smiled and said, "We will be here on the 3rd." And with that he stood, shook hands with John Chisum, and started back to the Slant BB ranch. Bill got back to the spread on the evening of the 14th and outlined the deal he had made with John Chisum. They had fourteen days to get everything in order, complete all branding, and get their herd on the trail for the seventy-five mile trek to Denton County.

Bill had thought about Chisum's stipulations as pertained to Betty not being welcome on the trail drive and had devised a plan in his mind. Bud and Kaede would accompany him with the herd to Denton County, and then Kaede would return to the spread, look after the ranch, and afford a level of protection for Betty. Bill and Bud would accompany the cattle on the drive to Fort Sumner, New Mexico. Bill figured, barring some unknown complications, he and Bud should be back to the ranch by the 10th of June.

The movement of the cattle from the ranch to Denton County was without incident. They left on the morning of March 28th and arrived late in the afternoon six days later on April 3rd. They held the small herd about a mile from the main herd and Bill rode in to report to John Chisum and get instructions for the trail branding operation. Chisum told him he would send a man out to do the tally of Bill's cattle and to furnish the trail branding iron and help with the branding operation. Bill thanked Chisum and returned to the herd.

The following morning Kaede shook hands with Bill and Bud and headed out on the two day ride back to the ranch and arrived without issue. Betty was happy to see him, and they had a nice evening meal together and discussed the work they needed to accomplish while Bill and Bud were gone.

The trail drive began on the morning of the 6th, one day later than planned because a small herd belonging to Frank Mistle was a day late due to flooding of a river they had to cross to get to Denton County. The area of West Texas was fairly desolate with lots of scrub, cactus, and rattlesnakes. Actually, the Chisum trail was much the same as the Goodnight/Loving trail for much of the drive. The drive took fifty-two days, and the specific route was dictated by the availability of grass and water.

The only mishap was a severe thunderstorm one night as they approached the New Mexico border which stampeded the herd and caused one cowboy to be thrown from his horse and trampled by the cattle. Michael Youngdale was the unfortunate young man's name. His body was recovered the next morning and brought to the trail camp. After the cattle were rounded up, the drovers dug a grave, and all gathered around while John Chisum read over the body from the Good Book.

They arrived at Fort Sumner on June 2, 1867 and received $7.25 a head for their cattle. Bill and Bud's share of the sale was $1,421.00 based on 196 head of cattle delivered at the sale site. Each individual owner shared the proportional loss of the cattle that either died or were lost on the drive.

Bill took his share of the sale, shook hands with John Chisum, and along with Bud, started back to their ranch in Hopkins County, Texas. They diverted somewhat and stopped in Dallas, Texas, for a couple days to purchase some new duds, get Betty a new dress, and purchase cartridges for their assorted rifles and pistols. Bill and Bud went to the Ervay Saloon to have a couple shots of rye, and an association which was to last for many years began.

The meeting was innocuous enough. Bud was approached by a pretty, blond haired young woman named Sara Bright who welcomed him and Bill to the Ervay. Bud was immediately infatuated. Bud and Sara engaged in conversation, and Bill excused himself and went across the street to their room at the Texas Star Hotel. Bud discovered that Sara had been married to a dentist named Fred Bright, and they had moved from St. Louis, Missouri, to Dallas, Texas, for him to start a dentistry practice. Shortly after they had arrived, they were walking down the boardwalk when shooting started in the street and a stray bullet hit Fred in the head. He died two days later. Henry Ervay, the saloon owner, was a kind and generous man and offered Sara a job as a hostess in the saloon. Bud and Sara got along well and discovered they had much in common. Bud spent the night in Sara's room above the saloon.

The next morning Bud took Sara to the Texas Star Hotel and had her wait in the lobby while he went to their room and got Bill. The three had breakfast at the Dallas House. After Bud promised Sara that he would come and visit with her as often as possible, he and Bill rode out of Dallas.

On the way back to Hopkins County, Bill and Bud stopped at some small homesteads and at one, bought a handsome mixed breed bull and three good looking heifers and drove them to their ranch to augment the Herefords in their permanent herd.

Kaede and Betty were delighted to see Bill and Bud, and everything fell back into a routine. The cowboys would gather cattle out of the bogs and started a selective breeding program to increase the quality of their beef cattle. Bud had another breeding program in mind and went to Dallas to see Sara once every month. In the fall of 1867, Bill and Bud were surveying their growing herd, and out of the blue, Bill said, "Bud, Sara seemed like a quality woman. It's none of my business, but you should either make her an honest woman or leave her alone so she can find a husband."

Bud said nothing but Bill could tell he was troubled. A couple days later, while the group was having dinner Bud announced, "I'm leaving for Dallas tomorrow morning to ask Sara to be my wife. If she says yes, we will get hitched, and I will be coming back in a few days with a wife."

Five days later Bud returned to the ranch driving a small four wheel carriage pulled by his horse with his saddle stored in the rear of the rig. After handshakes and embraces, Betty took Sara aside and helped her get her belongings into the small cabin. Betty looked at Bud and said, "I think you had better get busy building another cabin. This lady isn't going to share that cabin with three cowboys." Early the next morning, axes could be heard dropping trees to build another structure on the ranch.

Within three weeks there was a Baxter cabin on the spread, and Bud and Sara set up housekeeping. Sara and Betty shared the cooking duties, and the entire group met in the cooking and eating room for their meals. Bill Brubaker and Bud Baxter were beginning to see their dreams come to fulfillment. They owned 400 acres free and clear and had a couple thousand acres of public land to graze their cattle on.

If everything went well, there would be dozens of calves born in February or early March of 1868; be weaned by October, and ready to breed in December of 1869. By September 1870, their breeding process should be well established. They were no longer just cowboys; now they were cattlemen!

Chapter 14

The State of Texas came under military occupation (martial law) on August 20, 1866. With the advent of martial law, Hopkins County became part of the Fifth Military District. With the occupation of Texas, federal officials forced Anglos to accept immediate freedom for blacks as opposed to gradual and limited emancipation. Most white Southerners favored a gradual freedom for blacks, and Texans felt it was their right to decide the matter, not the federal government. Some Texans decided to fight back through covert activities. The Ku Klux Klan (KKK) was birthed and allowed the hooded members of the secret organization to intimidate, terrorize, and murder blacks and the Republicans who enforced the new rules.

The KKK continued to grow in power and political influence in Texas and by the end of 1867, virtually all of Texas experienced Klan or Klan-like terror. Thousands of blacks, Mexicans, recent European immigrants, federal loyalists, and even federal troops were systematically murdered by men hiding behind the anonymity of hoods.

During and after the Civil War, the black population of Hopkins County grew rapidly. Between 1861 and 1865, the black population of the county doubled because slaveholders from other areas of the south moved their slaves to Hopkins County to evade Union troops. By the end of the conflict, more than 2,000 blacks, or about one-fourth of the county population, lived in Hopkins County.

Not everyone agreed with the harshness and lawlessness of the KKK, but most county citizens had little regard or sympathy for its new black citizens. And if they did, were afraid of repercussions if they vocally shared their feelings.

****

In early November of 1867, Bill decided to spend the day surveying the range that he and Bud owned and looking for evidence of rustlers or other outlaw activity. Kaede had offered to ride along, but Bill wanted some time to himself to reflect on their growing cattle ranch and formulate plans in his mind for the next steps in the operation.

Bill believed in states' rights and had fought for the Confederacy during the Civil War, but he also believed in the rule of law. The horrible conflict was over, the blacks had been freed, and it was time to get on with life. He and Bud were making a good living, and the prospect of an even better economic status was within their reach. They didn't need a conflict.

When Bill got to the southeastern edge of his range, he topped a slight rise and saw five horsemen dragging a man behind one of the horses. Bill pulled out his Spencer and rode towards the men. When he got to within about 100 yards, he saw the men were wearing white hoods and pulling a black man. He spurred his horse, and when he got to with about fifty yards fired his rifle in the air and reined in his mount. The men stopped dragging the man, turned, and looked to see who had fired the shot. Bill ejected the spent shell, cocked the hammer, and hollered to the men, "What did that man do to deserve to be dragged to death?"

One of the men, since their faces were hidden, Bill couldn't tell which, hollered back, "He is a nigger who looked at a white woman, what other reason do we need? You need to get on with your business, Mister, before we decide to drag you some."

Bill bristled and said, "You might find I am a little harder to drag than a defenseless man. You are on my property, and this man is now under my protection. Release him and ride away, now."

The man on the far left raised his rifle and Bill shot him out of the saddle. His rifle hit the ground, and the other four men stayed still. Bill said, "I said leave, and now won't be too soon. You have one man with a bullet in him, this can get worse."

One of the men hollered, "You haven't heard the last of this, Mister. You will get a visit from us real soon."

"Thanks for the warning. Now I will return the favor. If I see a man on my property with a sack on his head, I will kill him on sight. Now get."

Two of the hooded men got down and loaded the wounded man on his horse and started to pick up the rifle, and Bill said, "Leave it. Get out of here."

The men rode away, and Bill trotted his horse to the black man, who was on the ground, his clothes in tatters, and bleeding from several scrapes and cuts. Bill took his canteen from the saddle pommel, dismounted, walked over to the man, and gave him a small drink of water. The man was alive but just barely, and his eyes were unfocused and bleary. Bill knew that Bud and the rest would be concerned if he didn't return in time for supper, but this man was in no condition to ride. Bill decided to make a fire and give the man some time to recover his strength and senses. He took the saddle off his horse, placed it under the man's head, and ground picketed the mount so that he could graze.

He had a cup and a bit of Arbuckle in his saddlebags, so he put some coffee grounds and water in the cup and placed it on the edge of the fire to boil. After the coffee was about the same color as the man he was helping, he moved the cup away from the fire with a glove, allowed it to cool a mite, and then gave the man a couple sips. After a couple minutes, the man perked up a little, and Bill gave him the cup and let him drink on his own.

When the man showed signs of being aware of his surroundings, Bill asked him his name. "Sir, my name if Wil Jefferson Byrd. I thank you for saving my life."

Bill introduced himself and asked Byrd if he thought he could ride double on the horse if he was helped up. Byrd allowed he could stay on the horse if Bill would help him get on. Bill saddled the horse, helped Byrd onto the horse, picked up the Henry rifle the Klansman had dropped, and then got in the saddle. Bill slowly and deliberately held the horse to a fast walk and arrived at the ranch yard just after sunset. Bud, Kaede, and the ladies came out and helped Byrd off the horse.

While Bill was recounting the story of finding the KKK dragging the black man, Betty and Sara took charge of Byrd and took him into the kitchen area and fixed him a plate of beef stew. While Byrd was eating, Betty cleaned his wounds and put some ointment on the worst of them. Bill got his mount rubbed down, gave the horse a scoop of grain, and washed off the man's blood and the trail dust. Bud and Kaede came in right after Bill finished cleaning up. After supper, Bill told Wil that he could sleep in the main cabin with him and Kaede and suggested that he should probably bed down and try to get some sleep, and they would try to find some decent clothes for him the next morning.

After Byrd went into the cabin the three cowboys discussed what they should do with regard to Mr. Byrd. Bill said, "Byrd is entitled to our protection as long as he is on our property. It may bring trouble to our door, but I don't think we have a choice."

Bud allowed Bill was right and they would do what they had to do when the time came and the KKK showed up at the ranch. Kaede said nothing but nodded his approval. He suspected the KKK wouldn't be fond of him either.

They felt that the KKK had all they wanted of the Slant BB and wouldn't be around for a few days but caution just made sense. They decided to split the darkness into three hour shifts until daylight. A week came and went. Wil Byrd was on the mend and worked hard on the ranch and ate enough to maybe make his work a break even deal. Bill felt that the hooded hoodlums would show up, but there was no way to project when it might occur. They just needed to stay ready.

Chapter 15

The cattlemen had no idea where the Ku Klux Klan members who were dragging Wil Byrd had come from, but they decided to go to Tarrant, Texas, to get some supplies. Bill allowed he would stay on the ranch and attend to some chores, and Bud and Kaede could go to Tarrant and get the items they needed for the ranch. Kaede placed the panniers on the pack horse, and they were ready to make the short trip.

Tarrant was about five miles farther than Sulphur Springs, but if they could get their supplies without incident, it would be worth the extra ride. Caney Creek was flooded, but they managed to get across without placing themselves or the horses in danger. They tied their horses to the hitching post in front of Miller's General Store and walked in and up to the counter. The owner, who was also the clerk, ignored them for a time, and Bud finally said, "Mister, we would like to purchase some supplies. Ten pounds of Arbuckle, ten pounds of bacon, and…"

At that point Frank Miller interrupted and said, "We don't have any coffee or bacon for sale." Bud looked at one of the shelves, and it contained several bags of Arbuckle coffee.

About that time, three rather tough looking men entered the store, and the man in front walked up to Bud and said, "You need to leave Tarrant; you have no friends here." The man then poked Kaede with his index finger and said, "We don't want Chinks or Niggers here in Tarrant."

Cat quick, Kaede grabbed the man's finger with his right hand and his elbow with his left and broke the man's finger and said, "Actually, I am Japanese, and you will have to pick your nose with your left hand for a while."

The man began cursing as one other man stepped forward, and Bud said, "You will do well to back off." Bud turned his attention to Miller and said, "You can sell us goods or not. It's your store, but if you want to keep it all in one piece, you need to call off your dogs."

Miller motioned for the men to leave and turned to Bud, "Your partner inserted himself in Ku Klux Klan business by helping the Nigger. If I sell anything to you, I would wake up with my store on fire. The Klan runs things around here."

Bud realized that he was barking up the wrong tree, turned, and walked out of the store followed by Kaede. They went back to the ranch and had a sit down with Bill and Wil and told them the short version of what they had encountered in Tarrant. They decided Bud and Bill would try to buy their supplies in Mount Pleasant, Texas, the next day. Maybe the store owner there wouldn't know them or wouldn't care who they were as long as their money was good.

The next morning Bill and Bud were off with the pack horse at daybreak and got to Mount Pleasant during the late evening. They took their horses to the livery, took their rifles, and went to the Dooley Café to have supper. After eating, they went down the street to the Mount Pleasant Hotel and checked in without incident.

The next morning they ate an early breakfast at Dooley's and went to the Titus General Store. There were a couple women in the store and Bill and Bud tipped their hats to them and walked to the counter. The clerk didn't smile but asked them what he could get for them. Bud placed their order for Arbuckle, bacon, beans, flour, salt, and sugar. Bill went to the clothing area and picked out a pair of boots, two pairs of cotton duck pants, suspenders, two cotton work shirts, a change of socks, and a hat and took them to the counter. When the clerk got their order together Bud started taking the supplies to the pack horse and Bill settled their bill.

The two women left the store and the clerk looked at Bill and said, "If asked, I am going to say that I didn't know who you were. If you want to buy supplies here again you will need to come at night. My wife and I live in the back. Just come to the back door and knock. I'm sorry, but I have a business to run here. If the Klan finds out I am selling you supplies, there will be hell to pay. You might want to know that there are rumors that the Klan plans to burn you out."

Bill shook the man's hand, thanked him for his kindness, and asked his name. The clerk said his name was Rufus Maxwell. As an afterthought, Bill decided to purchase two William Moore & Co. 10 gauge messenger shotguns and two boxes of buckshot. He paid for the weapons, joined Bud at the horses, and handed him one of the shotguns. Bill looked at Bud for a moment and said, "Looks like I have gotten us in a mess. If word of what I did has gotten to Titus County, we have to presume it is fairly well common knowledge in this part of Texas."

Bud looked at Bill and said, "You did what you had to do; no use crying over spilt milk. We have lived through much harder situations. Let's get back to the ranch before it gets completely dark."

Bill and Bud arrived around sunset, unsaddled their horses, carried the panniers to the kitchen area, and sat down to dinner. After dinner, the group discussed their circumstances with the Ku Klux Klan and decided that a constant vigil was warranted. They would continue the three hour shifts, but now, one of them would stand watch outside the buildings armed with a Moore 10 gauge shotgun. Kaede took the first shift, and everyone else turned in until their shift started.

As Bill and Bud were changing lookout shifts at 3 AM, they saw torch lights on the other side of creek in the far edge of the trees. Bill turned to Bud and said, "Better get everyone up and armed; looks like we are about to have company."

Bud came back in a couple minutes, and the two men separated so they wouldn't block shooting alleys if fireworks started. Bill was by the side of the corral, and Bud was beside the tool shed. Both men had one if the 10 gauge shotguns. Within minutes, fifteen men on horseback crossed the creek and rode into the cabin yard.

Bill called out from the corral and said, "You boys turkey hunting at night?" The men were startled and turned their horses toward Bill's voice.

Then Bud called out, "Bill, I think they are snipe hunting." Now the men realized they had ridden into a crossfire situation and were mighty uncomfortable.

Bill said, "No one has to die here tonight, but that is up to you folks. We aren't going to stay up all night until we are ole men waiting to see if you sheeters come to burn us out. I know you are cowards because you won't show your faces, but if one of you is stupid enough to go for a gun, we'll cut a few out of the herd."

A large man in the middle of the group called out, "We didn't come here to chew the fat. We're gonna burn you out, then run you out, and hang the Nigger. There are only two of them men; let's get um." With that, the Klansmen went for their guns, and Bill cut one in half with the shotgun and Bud did likewise to one on his side. The four rifles in the cabins opened up, and it sounded like a young war. The white sheets and torches made fine targets. Within just a few seconds, seven Klansmen were on the ground, and the rest raised their hands. Bill reloaded both barrels of his shotgun, cocked both hammers, and said, "Let those pistols fall to the ground and then start taking those flower sacks off your heads, and let's see who we have here." Bill had never seen any of the men before.

Bud spoke up and said, "Well, Mr. Miller, imagine finding you riding with these scum. I guess you lied about being afraid to sell us supplies. Get down and check the men on the ground to see if any of them are alive."

Miller checked each man in turn and turned to Bud and said, "Looks like five of them are dead, and the other two aren't in good shape. You men have won this battle, but you will lose the war. Every Klansman in Texas will be here to set this night right."

Bill walked up to Mr. Miller, looked him in the eye, and said, "Bud there is a pussycat and has a soft heart. If you sheeters ever come back, I will kill every man jack, drag you out into our pasture, and let the buzzards feed on your carcasses. Now tie the dead men across their saddles, put the wounded on their horses and get off this property; and I hope you have the good sense not to come back."

Bill and the crew had wounded three men and killed five in two encounters, and they hadn't a scratch. This wasn't to be the end of the conflict with the Klan, but it did put a stop to their visits to their ranch. The Klan would now take a more serendipitous approach to settling the score with the Slant BB.

Chapter 16

About noon the day following the Klan's night visit, Sheriff Jesse Davis and two deputies showed up at the Slant BB and said they had warrants for Bill Brubaker, Bud Baxter, and unnamed others for the murder of five men. Bill looked at the sheriff and said, "How are we to know that you aren't here on behalf of the hooded Klan members that were here last night? How are we to know the judge who issued this warrant wasn't here last night? No, I don't think we want to be arrested today. I tell you what; have Captain Chafee validate the propriety of the warrant and serve it, and we will surrender to him." The sheriff just looked at Bill and smiled a wry smile, turned his horse around, and the two deputies followed him across the creek, through the trees, and back towards Sulphur Springs.

Bill looked at Bud and said, "Something ain't right. That sheriff didn't push at all. He just turned around and left. If he was really here to serve a warrant, he would have dared us to resist arrest. For some reason his heart wasn't in it."

In the early afternoon Captain Adna R. Chaffee and a company of the United States 6th Calvary arrived. Bud looked at Bill and said, "What are we going to do now?"

Captain Chaffee reined in his horse and looked at Bill and said, "My compliments Captain Brubaker. Were all of you unscathed in the attack this morning?"

Bill looked at Captain Chafee and responded, "My compliments to you as well, Sir. Yes, Sir, we were fortunate; none of us were injured in the attack."

Captain Chaffee said, "You and Lieutenant Baxter did well to refuse to accompany the sheriff. One of my informants came to me and said that a group of Klansmen was going to wait at the far edge of the forest and assassinate the two of you from a hiding spot amongst the trees. I think the sheriff knew about the plot but wasn't happy to be involved. The Ku Klux Klan is a real problem around this part of Texas. Between chasing outlaws, Indians, and the KKK, I have my hands full. You folks put a big dent in their armor this morning."

Bill looked at Captain Chafee and said, "Then you aren't here to arrest us?"

Chaffee laughed and replied, "Heavens, no. When the informant told me what was going on, I came as fast as I could. If there was a medal for killing Klan scum I would award it to the two of you and your associates. Don't fret. The Klan can't testify against you without revealing their identity, and they are too cowardly for that. This incident is over, but you would do well to watch your back." With that, Captain Chafee tipped his hat, turned his horse and led the troopers back to the creek and across.

****

Adna Romanza Chaffee joined the Union Army in 1861 as a private and rose through the ranks to become a lieutenant general. He served in the Civil War, Indian Wars, Spanish-American War, and the Boxer Rebellion in China. He served as the Chief of Staff of the United States Army from 1904 to 1906. Chafee died November 1, 1914, in California, and his body was transported to Arlington Cemetery in Virginia and was buried with honors.

****

Bill, Bud, and the rest of the crew met in the kitchen and discussed the events of the day. The Klan would love to murder all of them for killing five of their fellow sheeters. The Klan's problem was too much federal presence, and the Slant BB was well fortified. If the Klan went after the Slant BB it might bring in more federal troops and the KKK would lose all its influence in this part of Texas. Also, a frontal attack on the Slant BB would no doubt result in more dead or wounded Klansmen.

The Slant BB men decided that the Klan was extremely unlikely to harm the women. Even people who looked the other way when the Klan terrorized blacks and Mexicans wouldn't tolerate their harming white women. With that decided and Betty and Sara well-armed, the cowboys decided it was time to get back to the business of rounding up cattle.

The next morning, Bill, Bud, Kaede, and Wil headed out to the bogs to search for longhorn cattle to build the herd. They only took a short break for some hardtack and coffee at mid-day and managed to get back to the spread with thirteen cows in tow, not a bad day's work. Wil had rarely ridden a horse, and that was an ancient plow horse, before working with Bill and Bud, but took to the saddle like a seasoned cowboy. When Bill had asked Wil if he was willing to work on the ranch for $25.00 a month and found, it brought tears to his eyes. He looked at Bill with misty eyes and said, "I can never repay you for your kindness in saving my life and now in giving me a job.

Bill looked at Wil and replied, "You are not in my debt; stopping the Klan from dragging you to death was the right thing to do. As to "giving" you a job, I'm not giving you anything. You will earn every penny I pay you and more. You are part of the Slant BB family and crew now."

It was approaching Christmas of 1867, and Betty and Sara were decorating, baking cookies, and bear sign in preparation for the celebration. As they were working in the kitchen preparing the evening meal, Sara fainted. Betty got a damp cloth and placed it on her head, and after she came around, she got her to her feet. She looked at Betty and said, "I have been getting sick every morning for the past couple weeks and I get lightheaded. I'm reasonably sure that I am pregnant."

"Have you told Bud?"

"No, I wanted to be sure before I got his hopes up. I guess I am now sure. Let's keep this to ourselves, and I will tell him and everyone else when we have our Christmas dinner."

Bill decided that he would ride over to Mount Pleasant and visit Titus General Store to buy a comb

102

and brush set for Betty for Christmas and some rock candy. He arrived well after dark, and as requested, he went to the rear of the store and knocked on Mr. Maxwell's door. In a few seconds, Maxwell came to the door and asked Bill to come in, introduced him to Mrs. Maxwell, and said, "Let's go into the store and get you the things you need." While Bill was looking at rock candy, he spied a tin on a shelf which said chocolate. He turned to Rufus and asked, "What is chocolate?"

Maxwell looked at him, smiled, and said, "The best thing I have ever put in my mouth. This tin came all the way from Bern, Switzerland, and is produced by a man named Jean Tobler."

"How much is it?"

"Expensive, Mr. Brubaker, that little tin is $1.00, but it is worth every penny if you have a sweet tooth and the money."

Bill bought the tin of chocolate, a comb and brush set with little flowers on the brush, and one pound of rock candy then thanked Rufus Maxwell for his kindness. Bill went out the back door of the store, placed the candy and gift in his saddle bags, mounted his horse and went down the alley to the main street leading out of town. He got about fifty yards, and a man hollered, "Hey, you're the son of a bitch who shot my brother at your ranch."

Bill cocked both barrels of his messenger shotgun and turned his horse to face the man. People began boiling out of saloons on both sides of the street to see what all the commotion was about. There were gas lights about every fifty or so feet along both sides of the street, so there was no problem in seeing Bill or the man who had hollered.

Bill looked at the man and said, "I have no idea who your brother is or if he survived. There were fifteen men with hoods on, they drew down on us, and got what they deserved."

The man sneered and said, "I'm Fester Johnson and my brother Herman lost his right arm to one of your bullets."

"Don't know him, and though I didn't shoot him, that makes no difference. They came to my spread looking for trouble and got it; I own the place, so it is my responsibility."

"I'm going to kill you, Brubaker."

"No, no you're not, but your brother is going to outlive you if you don't turn around and walk away. I have no desire to kill you, but that is your choice, not mine."

The man fidgeted and shifted from one foot to the other and said, "I have called you out. I have to do this, or I am a coward."

"Son, if you go for that hog leg, you will die on this street tonight with your guts scattered all over the dirt. This has nothing to do with you being brave or a coward; it has to do with being smart. Do yourself a favor and choose to stay alive."

Johnson fidgeted some more and said, "It ain't worth it. I'm gonna go have a drink." With that, he turned and walked away. Bill watched Johnson walk away, uncocked the hammers of the shotgun, and pulled his Spencer out of its scabbard just in case he changed his mind after he got out of shotgun range. He didn't.

Bill got back to the ranch around two in the morning, and after taking the saddle off, rubbing down the horse, and putting him in the corral, quietly took his saddle bags into the cabin and hit the sack. As he lay awake, he thought, "We are celebrating the birth of a baby who came into the world to bring peace and love. I gave my Christmas gift tonight by letting that boy in Mount Pleasant live. This is going to be a wonderful Christmas."

Chapter 17

The Christmas dinner was a really great meal. Wil had gone hunting and killed a fine gobbler which he cleaned, and Betty and Sara prepared. The two ladies had baked apple and pecan pies. Bill and Bud had butchered a young steer, and the ladies had made a large roast. They also had beans which had been cooked from dried beans from the Titus store.

Bill stood to make a toast, and everyone raised their glass. "Here's to good friends, health, and future success."

When Bill sat back down, Sara stood and said she had an announcement to make: "Bud and I are going to have a baby in the spring." Everyone was hooting and hollering, but Bud looked like he had swallowed an entire plug of tobacco. He recovered his normal color in a minute or so, hugged Sara and smiled sheepishly.

The Slant BB crew lay around the spread until after New Year's Day 1868, and then began their round up efforts again. At last count, Bill had estimated they had just under 200 cattle on the ranch or on grazing land adjoining the property. The bulls were doing their job, and many cows were fairly heavy with calves and would be calving in February or early March. Bill figured the herd would grow by about seventy-five calves by the middle of March. He kinda chuckled and thought to himself that the crew was going to increase by at least one in April or May.

By the end of April the cowboys had rounded up another 120 strays and branded them. Bill's count of the new calves was pretty close. He had counted seventy-one on his rides around the ranch. He also found two still-born calves. He had no idea of how many more calves were on the grazing land, but he and the others needed to take a branding iron, start searching for the new calves, and get them branded. The men went out in twos, Bill and Wil and Bud and Kaede to find and brand new calves. After a week, the tally came to 436 head of cattle, more or less.

Bill and Bud talked over the cattle operation and decided it was time to drive some of the cattle to Fort Arbuckle in Garvin County, Oklahoma. They figured the calves would be weaned by the end of September. They decided that Bill would ride to Fort Arbuckle and test the water on selling some cattle to the fort, and since Sara was nearing having the baby, Bud would hang around the ranch while Wil and Kaede would keep rounding up strays.

****

Fort Arbuckle was established in April 1851, by Company D of the 5th United States Army Infantry. Many people thought the fort may have been named after Arbuckle coffee, but General Matthew Arbuckle, who was the Commander of the Military Department of Missouri, had the distinction of the fort being named after him. After the Civil War, the purpose of the fort was to protect the "Civilized" Indians, mostly Chickasaw and

Choctaw, from the raiding Kiowa and Comanche. It was also a way-station and housed Sutler's store, a resupply depot for prospectors on their way to the California gold fields. In 1868, the fort was occupied by the Army's 10th U. S. Cavalry known as the "Buffalo Soldiers."

****

Charles and John Arbuckle founded Arbuckle coffee. Prior to their method of roasting coffee beans, coffee was sold green, and the cowboy had to roast the beans in a skillet over a campfire. After roasting, the coffee beans had to be ground, no small task while on the trail. If a single bean was burned, the entire batch had to be discarded. Arbuckle roasted the beans, ground them, and then packed the coffee in metal containers. About 1866, Arbuckle added a sugar and egg glaze on the coffee beans after roasting, packaged them in one-pound packages, and shipped them to stores across the west.

****

On May 27th in 1868, Sara Baxter gave birth to Mattie Lea Baxter, a bouncing baby girl with red hair and a loud voice. Bill knew nothing of the birth of Mattie because he was near the Oklahoma border. It was around 200 miles from Hopkins County, Texas, to Fort Arbuckle and Bill figured he could make it in six days if he didn't dally. Everything went well until he got into Oklahoma. Southern Oklahoma was a rocky land filled with arroyos, hills, and valleys. Bill camped about ten miles into Oklahoma and didn't build a fire.

When Bill awoke he heard a bird call that immediately alerted him. This bird had an echo to its voice, which meant that it wasn't a bird but some human trying to imitate a bird call. Bill got his Spencer and coach gun and crawled into the rocks near the campsite. He didn't have to wait long. A Kiowa warrior came running and screaming towards him and Bill shot him with the messenger shotgun. Then all hell broke loose.

The Kiowa shot Bill's horse. Then another brave charged, and Bill shot him with the second barrel of the messenger shotgun. As near as Bill could determine, there were six or seven braves in the war party; he had killed two of them which would leave four or five. There was no way that he could protect himself from that many Indians if they all charged at once but for some reason they didn't.

Suddenly, Bill felt a sharp sting in his right calf and looked, and there was an arrow protruding from both sides of his lower leg. When he looked in the direction of the fletched end of the arrow, he saw an Indian moving between the rocks. Bill pointed the Spencer and waited for the Indian to move again. He didn't have to wait long before the brave stood to shoot another arrow. When the hostile exposed himself, Bill shot him in the gut.

Two Kiowa were dead and another gut-shot; that left three or four Indians. Bill took out his Bowie, cut the arrow near the entry point, grasped the arrowhead, jerked and the arrow came free. The arrow hadn't hit the bone or an artery and was only slowly seeping blood. If he didn't get an infection, he would be all right. He took a couple sips of water and waited to see what would happen next. There was nothing. No movement, just silence.

Bill Brubaker had survived the entire Civil War without so much as a scratch, and now he was pinned down with a hole in his leg and a dead horse. After about an hour, Bill saw movement off to his right about 150 feet away. He aimed his Spencer in the general direction of the movement and waited and waited. After several minutes, he saw an arm extend and motion for unseen Indians to move to the left. Bill shot the arm and was rewarded by a scream. After the Indian screamed another Indian stood and aimed a Sharps carbine, fired, and missed Bill by inches. Bill took quick aim, fired, and hit the brave in the groin area. Two hostiles were dead, two badly wounded, and one with an arm wound of unknown severity. There were either one or two uninjured Kiowa still hiding in the rocks.

Bill lay still for hours waiting for the other one or two Indians to do something. Finally he saw the body of the gut-shot Indian being dragged between rocks and held his fire. Then the Indian he had shot in the groin area limped away using his rifle as a crutch. In a few minutes, he heard the sound of horses as the Kiowa left.

Bill had survived the Kiowa attack with only the one wound. The problem was that he was many miles from civilization in any direction and now had ·

no transportation. He figured it was about 100 miles to Fort Arbuckle. The problem was that there was nothing but rough country between where he was and the fort. Bill was in real trouble.

Bill took the saddle off the dead horse and slung it across his shoulder, placed the Spencer in its scabbard, tucked the shotgun under his arm, and started walking north. His leg was beginning to ache more and more with each step, and he knew there was no way he was going to be able to walk all the way to Garvin County, Oklahoma. Quitting just wasn't part of Bill's makeup. He was going to walk on until his last breath left him.

Bill stopped for the night in a small arroyo and slept like the dead. The following morning, he started out again. Around mid-day, he was exhausted and out of water. He sat down in the shade of a large rock and decided to rest for a spell. As he lay back on the saddle, he heard the sound of approaching horses. There was no place to go, and he didn't have the strength to try and get away anyway. He just lay still and waited. In a couple minutes a small party of Comanche appeared led by One Eye. Bill was never so happy to see an Indian.

One Eye got down off his horse and gave Bill his canteen. As Bill was drinking, he noticed that one of the Comanche was Small Eagle, the Indian that he and his group had nursed and taken out at night to avoid the Apache. Small Eagle smiled at Bill and nodded his head. Small Eagle started a fire, and Bill took out his cup and put some water and Arbuckle grounds in it and placed it beside the fire to boil.

Small Eagle examined the wound on Bill's leg and said, "You lucky my friend; the arrow didn't hit bone." Small Eagle made a paste with some dried powder he was carrying in his bag and water, applied some on both sides of the wound, and then bound the leg with cloth and a couple pieces of rawhide.

One Eye and his party stayed the night, and the next morning gave Bill one of the extra ponies they had stolen on their raid. Bill noticed there was no brand on the horse, so he assumed it had been stolen from other Indians even though the horse was shod. Perhaps the horse had been taken from a wagon train headed for the gold fields in California. Bill really didn't care; it was a horse. One Eye looked at Bill and said, "We are even now. You helped Small Eagle and now we have helped you. Next time we meet, I will kill you." With that bit of encouraging news, One Eye mounted and rode off with his band of Comanche.

Bill made it to Fort Arbuckle without further incident and reached an agreement with the fort commander, Captain Stedman Reed, to provide seventy-five head of cattle at a price of $7.30 per head. Bill promised delivery of the cattle by the 15th of November. The money for the cattle would pay Kaede and Will for a year and give the Slant BB money for supplies without having to go into their savings.

When Bill got back to the Slant BB ranch, he was greeted by Bud, Sara, and an infant named Mattie who was to become the apple of his eye and he would become her god-father.

Bill and Wil took the seventy-five head of cattle to Fort Arbuckle without incident. When Bill got the cash for the cattle, he talked to Wil and asked him if he wanted to enlist in the Army since there were black soldiers at the fort. Wil looked at Bill, smiled, and said, "You trying to get rid of me?" They traveled back to Hopkins County and the ranch without incident.

The herd continued to grow and so did the Baxter family. Sara gave birth to James Budwell Baxter (BJ), Jr on July 1, 1870. Then Nathan Forrest Baxter was born on August 30, 1871; and finally, William Huzzah Baxter on December 30, 1872.

When the calendar turned to 1873, Bill and Bud were the owners of around 1,000 head of Texas longhorn and mixed breed cattle. Bud had three sons and a daughter, and life was wonderful. Betty was now about eighteen or nineteen years old, and life on the ranch was drastically changing.

Chapter 18

The day after New Year's marked the end of holiday celebrations, and it was time to get back into the swing of things. Bill was sitting on the porch of the original cabin smoking his pipe when Betty walked up and sat down on the edge of the deck. Nothing was said for a few minutes. Finally Betty turned, looked at Bill, and said, "Have you noticed that I'm not the little girl Bud found in the swamp?"

Bill was taken aback. He had noticed that Betty had filled out in all the right places and had become a beautiful woman, but he somehow still saw her as a child. He kinda stuttered and stammered and finally said, "Yes, I know you have grown up."

Betty smiled and said, "Here's the deal, Captain Brubaker. I have loved you since I was a little girl. I'm tired of waiting for you to recognize that I am now a woman. I have seen the way you look at me when you think I'm not looking. Either you get off your duff and marry me, or I want you to take me to Dallas so that I can find a husband and have my own family. I'm tired of loving Sara's children; I want children of my own." With that, Betty got up and walked to her quarters leaving Bill with his mouth open.

Bill had been focused on building a ranch, breeding cattle, and trying to fulfill his dreams and had never considered marriage as part of the deal. Now he was faced with a decision. He had feelings for Betty and had always loved her, but more as a younger sister. Now that younger sister relationship was out the window, and he had a decision to make.

The next day, Bill and Bud were discussing their plans for the rest of the year when out of the blue, Bud looked at Bill, smiled, and asked, "So, partner, are you going to marry Betty? Don't look so surprised. This is a small group. Word gets around, and Betty and Sara have no secrets from each other. She told Sara about her ultimatum to you."

Bill smiled and replied, "I have thought on it all night, and I love that gal. And yes, I am going to marry her."

The following day, Bill rode to Mount Pleasant, talked to the Methodist minister and asked if he would perform a marriage ceremony for him. Bill had established a great deal of good-will and respect in Mount Pleasant by allowing Fester Johnson to live when the young man accosted him. Reverend Jacob Smith allowed he would be happy to perform the ceremony and asked if he had a date in mind. Bill thought for a minute and said, "How would the first Saturday in February work for you, Reverend Smith?" The reverend said that would be fine. Bill followed up by asking if it would be too much of an imposition for the reverend to come to the ranch to perform the ceremony. Reverend Smith said he would be honored, and Bill said they would be happy to pick him up with a carriage and take him back home after the ceremony. The reverend said he appreciated the offer, but that he would use his own carriage and leave after the ceremony so as not to make someone miss the festivities.

With the date of the marriage set, Betty asked Bud to take her and Sara to Mount Pleasant so that she could buy a wedding dress. The next day was very cold, and Sara begged off because she didn't want the baby out in the bad weather. Bud and Betty took off in the buggy and went to the dry goods store in Mount Pleasant. There wasn't a white dress in the store, so Betty settled on a light pink dress with flowers and a cream colored Bollman hat with a small brim. Bud went to the saloon and bought two bottles of Rye whiskey with the seals still attached.

On the first Saturday in February, Reverend Smith appeared at the Slant BB right on schedule and performed the marriage ceremony. Betty Jean Wilson was now Mrs. William Brubaker. The celebration went well into the night, and Bill and Betty spent the night in the first cabin after evicting Kaede and Wil who slept in the kitchen area. The next morning, Bill and Betty left for Dallas in the carriage. The trip was leisurely, and they spent three days and nights to cover the seventy-five miles, stopping at small settlements or trading posts each night. Dallas was great with its theaters, restaurants, and fine hotels. They spent five days in Dallas, eating in the finest restaurants, doing some shopping, and then returned to Hopkins County, stopping at the same places on the way back.

The next priority was getting another cabin built for Bill and Betty. Bill had bought a second wood cook stove in Dallas to augment the one in the kitchen area which both Betty and Sara appreciated greatly. The mercantile store promised the stove would be ready for pick-up within two weeks. It took three weeks to get the cabin built and another week for Bud to make the furniture. By the last of March, the cabin was completed Betty had her own stove, and took up housekeeping in her own home.

Late in the afternoon on November 8, 1873, Betty went into labor. Sara was ready when Betty's water broke and had boiling water and lots of clean sheets ready. Betty was in labor with her first child for a little more than five hours, and Bill was a nervous wreck. As Bill was pacing outside the cabin, he heard a baby cry, and a few moments later Sara walked out on the porch with a little bundle and said, "Mr. Brubaker, meet Mr. Brubaker." Bill had a son. The boy was named Frederick William Brubaker, Frederick after his paternal grandfather, and William after his father. He would be called Freddie while a child.

On September 12, 1874, Freddie, who was to later be called Fred, gained two sisters: Mary Francis and Carrie Marie Brubaker. There were now seven children running or crawling around the Slant BB ranch, and Bill and Betty decided three was enough for them.

Bill and Bud decided that in late October, after calves were weaned, they would take 1,000 head of cattle to Kansas. They discussed which of them should accompany the herd and which one should stay to attend to the day to day operations of the ranch. Bill drew the long straw and was to go with the herd. The problem was, the drive was about 500 miles, and they would need a chuck wagon, cook, and some drovers.

Bill went to Mount Pleasant and took Kaede along, bought a Conestoga wagon, and had Kaede outfit it with supplies that would be needed for the nearly two month drive. Bill walked across the street to the Salty Dog Saloon and announced he needed drovers for two months of trail work to Kansas. Several men came forward, and after talking to each one individually, selected Fester Johnson, the young man whose life he had spared, Jason Kimmel, Josh Ramsey, and an old hand named Honks Pickens. The men were told to be at the Slant BB the next morning; they would brand all the cattle which were unmarked and leave in three days. Johnson lingered behind and thanked Bill for letting him go on the drive and for allowing him to live when he had a snoot full and acted like an idiot. Bill told him not to worry about it; everyone did things they regretted.

Kaede wasn't happy about having the cooking duties placed on him, and Bill, sensing his displeasure, told him he would get double wages for the two months on the trail drive. The younger drovers would receive $25.00 a month, Honks $27.50 because of his experience, and Wil his regular pay and all the trail dust he could eat. Bill also hired a new ranch hand to help Bud while he, Wil, and Kaede were away. His name was Dusty Jones, and he had a limp but was a good worker.

Bill hated to leave Betty with three small children, two only a month old, but he had little choice. Bud had four small children, so it would be the same predicament if Bud went. He felt comfortable with Bud in charge of the ranch and there to protect the families. They pulled out on October 27, 1874, and headed for Dodge City, Kansas, with 1,003 head of longhorn cattle.

Chapter 19

The Chisholm Trail was named after Jesse Chisholm and was the major route from Texas to the Kansas cattle buyers. The trail was only used from 1867 to 1884 but was instrumental in helping the impoverished state of Texas recover from the Civil War.

When the Civil War ended, Texas' only potential asset was it countless longhorn cattle which had been roaming free during the war years. The East had developed a liking to beef, and a man named Joseph G. McCoy persuaded Kansas Pacific railroad officials to lay a siding at the small town of Abilene, Kansas. He began building holding pens and loading facilities and sent word to Texas cowmen that a cattle market was available if they would drive the livestock to Abilene.

The market suffered a glut of beef cattle in 1871 which lowered the price. The market would rebound as cattle were taken to different markets. The Trail started at the North Canadian River in Indian Territory and continued 220 miles to Wichita, Kansas. The Chisholm Trail was initially referred to as only the Trail, Kansas Trail, or Abilene Trail. Although the Trail applied only to that part of the trail north of the Red River, Texas cowmen applied Chisholm's name to the entire trail from the Rio Grande to central Kansas.

After 1871, the Trail branched to Ellsworth, Junction City, Newton, and Wichita. The western Trail ended at Dodge City, Kansas.

The cattle drive went without incident. The Red River was forded without the loss of cattle, chuck wagon, or drovers. The Chisholm Trail wasn't really a trail as such. Other than using a common fording at river crossings, cattle would spread out, sometimes over a mile, to graze as they walked along. The secret to driving cattle to market was to let them eat as much grass as possible on the trip so they could maintain or increase their weight. Ten to twelve miles a day was the objective, and so far, Bill and the drovers were maintaining that pace.

Moving cattle during the winter was a miserable job. The air was cold, and there was a constant wind which would chill to the bone. Before crossing the Red River, Bill went to Doan's Store and posted a note to Betty telling her that they were making good time and had encountered no difficulties. After crossing the Red, Bill and the crew pushed the cattle into Indian Territory (Oklahoma). Other than a couple of troublemakers, the herd was well behaved and followed an old longhorn steer that was at least fifteen years old and had a horn span of more than seven feet.

Meanwhile back at the ranch, because of the cold weather, the children had to spend far too much time in the cabins and were driving Betty and Sara crazy. Bud and Dusty were breaking mustangs when Bud saw riders in the distance coming towards the ranch. He hollered at Dusty and said, "Dusty, let's go to the cabins and get our rifles just in case these riders

121

are trouble." With that, Bud went to his cabin and alerted Betty and Sara who got out their Henry repeating rifles and got the children situated on the floor in the back of the Baxter cabin. Dusty went to the bunkhouse and got his rifle. Betty stood at the east window, and Sara took the same position in her cabin.

In about fifteen minutes six men rode into the ranch yard with an ox drawn two wheeled cart following them. Bud was sitting on the porch holding his cocked ten gauge messenger shotgun in his lap. The men were rough looking and a mixture of Mexicans, Indians, and one Anglo. Bud waited until they all stopped and asked them what they wanted. The Mexican nearest Bud said, "Gringo, we want to water our horses."

Bud pointed towards the copse of trees and said, "The creek is right over there; help yourselves to all the water you want."

The Mexican didn't move and was looking at all the buildings and said, "You have a nice place; where are all your ranch hands?"

"The ones who don't shoot very well are driving cattle to Kansas. The ones who shoot very well are in the cabins, standing by the windows with rifles."

The Mexican laughed and said, "Gringo, I think you lie. I think it is just you and two women."

Bud looked at the Mexican for a moment and replied, "You think what you want, but you need to go to the creek, water your horses, and move on." With that, the Mexican reached for his pistol, and

Bud shot him out of the saddle with the messenger shotgun. One of the Indians charged his horse at the cabin on his left, and Dusty Jones shot him with his rifle. When the other riders went for their weapons, Betty and Sara opened up with their rifles, and two more riders fell out of their saddles. Bud got out of his chair and shot another of the men with the shotgun. That left one rider and the man driving the team pulling the wagon. Both men dropped their guns and put up their hands.

Bud looked at the two men and said, "Climb down and start loading those men on the wagon."

The driver said, "This man isn't dead."

"Then put him on the wagon alive. Just get them loaded and get off this ranch, or you can join your friends." The two men loaded the three dead men and the two wounded individuals into the wagon and started towards the creek and trail through the trees. Dusty came out of the cabin and said, "What the heck was that all about?"

Bud said, "That, my young friend was Comancheros, a nasty bunch who would have killed us then taken the women and children to Mexico and sold them." Betty and Sara were upset with having possibly killed the men, but they realized that, on the frontier, sometimes it was kill or be killed, or worse.

****

Bill and Wil were riding alongside the herd separated by about fifty feet, and Bill said, "Wil, don't turn and look, but we are being shadowed by a man on the ridge over your shoulder."

"I saw him earlier; he has been trailing us for some time. I wonder when he and his partners will try to cut the herd."

"Probably tonight or real early in the morning. Get Honks and let's get our heads together on how to handle this." In a few minutes, Wil came back with Honks and the three of them sat on their horses and discussed the situation.

Bill said, "There are six of us. I want two men with the herd all night; we will switch turns every three hours. Try to keep the cows tightly packed and that will make it harder to cut a few without us hearing them. Keep saddles on the horses all night. Just loosen the cinches so they will be as comfortable as possible."

About 2 AM, Bill awoke to the sound of gunfire. It took a moment for him to get his senses going; then he jumped up, pulled the cinch tight on his horse, and headed for the herd. Three drovers were right on his heels. Fester and Jason were exchanging pistol shots with three or four men and trying to keep their horses under control. Bill pulled his Spencer, took aim, squeezed off a round, and one of the rustlers fell off his horse. The other two rode away into the darkness.

Bill rode over to Fester and Jason and asked if they were all right. Fester spoke up and said, "Not a scratch boss; you sure can shoot that rifle."

The entire crew was together now, and Bill turned to the group and said, "It's early, but we would be leaving anyway in a couple hours so let's get the herd started. Kaede will get us some grub when we get settled in a nice open space where we can see a good distance." With that, they headed the cattle out towards the north.

Bill rode over and checked on the man he had shot and discovered he was still alive but carrying a piece of lead in his shoulder. Bill helped the man get on his horse and then told him, "Tell your friends that dying isn't a good plan for stealing cattle. You folks hit us again and I will personally come after you, chase you to hell if I have to, and then hang you." They had no more trouble with that group of rustlers!

Well into Indian Territory Bill was approached by seven Apache. The leader walked his horse up to Bill and said, "Are you the one called Brubaker?" Bill nodded in the affirmative. The Apache then said, "We are traveling with our women and children. I hoped you would give us a cow, so we don't have to steal one and maybe someone gets killed."

Bill looked at the Apache and asked, "Are you with Gray One?"

The Apache looked grim and responded, "No, I am called *Itza-chu*, Great Hawk in your tongue. Your soldiers killed Gray One about two months ago."

Bill looked at Great Hawk and said, "Not my soldiers, and, yes, you can have a beef cow. I will get my trail boss to cut you out one and bring it to you." Great Hawk thanked Bill, turned his horse, and headed back towards their camping area. Honks cut out one of the cows that looked haggard and drove it to the Indian camp and then returned to the herd.

The rest of the drive went well, and on December 16, 1874, Bill sold 989 head of longhorn cattle to the Thomas Sutter Company in Dodge City, Kansas, for $21.00 a head. He had Mr. Sutter issue him a check for $20,000.00 and give him $769.00 in cash so he could pay the drovers. He and Bud had been right about the winter market being better than the summer. Their herd was the only one in Dodge City. Now all he had to do was travel 500 miles in nine days to get home for Christmas. Bill paid off the drovers, sold the Conestoga wagon, and he, Wil, and Kaede lit out for Hopkins County, Texas, leading two horses each.

Honks, Jason, Fester, and Josh decided they would stay in Dodge for a few days, drink a little whiskey, and sample the wares of a couple soiled doves before starting back to the ranch.

Chapter 20

Bill, Kaede, and Wil made the trip back to Hopkins County, Texas, in seven days and arrived at the Slant BB ranch on the afternoon of December 24, 1874, dead tired and with extremely chaffed hind ends but happy. Bill and Bud were finally financially solvent. In 1874, $20,000.00 was a lot of money, and with their other savings, they had close to $23,000.00. Bill and Bud were wealthy cattlemen by the standards of the 1870s.

Christmas of 1874 was a triple celebration: Christmas, having Bill, Kaede, and Wil back, and the sale of the cattle. Bud had gone to Mount Pleasant and bought rag dolls for each of the girls, tinplate toys for Nathan and William, and as requested by Bill, a small saddle for BJ. They enjoyed a feast of ham, turkey, and apple and cherry pies from dried fruit Bud had bought from Maxwell's store. Dusty Jones went to Mount Pleasant to spend the Christmas holiday with his older sister and her husband.

On January 4, 1875, Bill left for Dallas to open an account with the Texas State Bank, one of thirteen national banks in Texas at the time. One of the requirements of the new national banks was that they had to have at least $50,000.00 in deposits at all times. Bill opened a joint account in the name of William Travis Brubaker and James Budwell Baxter. After completing that piece of business, Bill went to the Dallas Emporium and bought a blue dress for Sara and a light green dress for Betty.

When Bill returned from Dallas, he and Bud discussed the movement of cattle. They were moving what they considered breeding stock to the east side of the ranch and cattle for market to the west. They're plan was to segregate the cattle and drive them to Montana. This was to be an enormous undertaking because it was around 1,700 miles from Hopkins County, Texas, to southeastern Montana. The route would take them through Indian Territory, Kansas, Nebraska, and eastern Wyoming before finally ending up in Montana. Bill and Bud had been told there was free land in Montana and rich grasslands for grazing cattle. They figured the trip would take about six months and if they left in the early spring of 1875, they should be able to arrive in Montana around the middle of August. This would give them sufficient time to build shelters before the winter season began.

People would later ask Bill and Bud why they decided to leave a fine ranching operation in Texas and take their families all the way to Montana. During the 1870s, Hopkins County was becoming inundated with farmers who were raising grain crops, planting orchards, and raising cotton. All the "free graze" land adjacent to the 400 acres owned by the Slant BB was slowly being gobbled up by homesteaders. Bill and Bud discussed their options. They could have fought the homesteaders and tried to run them out as did some of their fellow ranchers. They figured the homesteaders had as much right to the land as they did. And after all, Bill and Bud started life on farms in Missouri and had a soft spot for hard working farmers. Therefore, they decided to opt for building a new ranch in Montana Territory.

Certainly there were inherent dangers in moving cattle and families across the Great Plains. But Bill and Bud had their dream of building a large and prosperous ranch and it would never materialize in Texas under the prevailing circumstances.

Bill and Bud got the entire group together and discussed their plans. The kids were excited about the adventure but really couldn't comprehend the great distance to Montana. Betty and Sara knew this was Bill and Bud's dream, and they were happy to be supportive of the adventure. Kaede said that he was homesick for Japan and thought if he went to Montana, he would never see his homeland again. He decided he would go back to Japan after helping get the trip in order.

A couple weeks later, after hugs, handshakes, and a few tears, Kaede rode off towards Dallas. Once he arrived, he went to the livery, talked to the hostler, and made a deal to sell him his horse and saddle for $130.00. He then walked to a general store and sold his Henry rifle, pistol and holster. Presuming he made it to Japan, he wouldn't need the weapons.

Kaede stayed overnight in the livery and caught the morning train to Galveston. The train was hot, cramped, and uncomfortable. He ate two meals at roadhouses near the train depot on short water stops. The first meal was all right, the second gave him the squirts and he spent a day running back and forth to the Hopper Toilet which was nothing more than a hole in the floor of the train which allowed human excrement to fall on the tracks as the train moved along.

Kaede found a tramp steamer in Galveston that was making deliveries to South America, then around Cape Horn, and on to California. He talked to the captain about working in the kitchen for his fare and an agreement was made.

****

A trip from the Gulf of Mexico around Cape Horn could take three to six months. Storms often made the trip miserable. Passengers and crew ate salt preserved meats, fish, dried beans, rice, and potatoes. One of the staples was called lobscouse, a hash made of salted meat, potatoes, and sea biscuits softened in water. To make water more palatable, a concoction called switchel which added molasses, vinegar, and spices was used. Bugs always invaded the flour stores, and mold and insects were constant food companions.

****

In San Francisco, Kaede caught passage on a Pacific Mail Steamship going to Hong Kong and paid $30.00 for a steerage class ticket. The conditions were horrible with little privacy, bad food, and poor sanitation, but Kaede survived the crossing. The ocean voyage had taken thirty-four miserable days. The ship docked at Victoria Harbor, and Kaede immediately started looking for a ship headed for

Japan. After a couple attempts, he found another tramp steamer headed to Fukuoda, Japan, by way of Formosa to drop trade goods, and then through the East China Sea.

Once he got off the ship in Fukuoda he caught rides to his village of Dazaifu. Kaede's parents and extended family were delighted to see him back home, and best of all, his childhood girlfriend, Niko, had not married. Kaede Higa rectified that situation within two months.

****

Wil allowed that the only family he had was the Baxter's and Brubaker's. Wil assumed his parents were dead and had no idea where his siblings might be, so if they were willing, he would tag along. Bill spoke for the group and said, "Wil, we think of you as family as well; you know you are welcome to come along." Dusty Jones allowed he would go if they wanted him along. His parents were deceased, and other than his sister, he had no ties to Hopkins County, Texas. Bill said he would go to Mount Pleasant and leave word that if Kimmel, Ramsey, and Pickens wanted to make the trip to Montana to come to the ranch.

Bill and Bud, with the aid of their wives, were making a list of things that they were going to take on the trip. This move meant leaving their home and moving half way across the country lock, stock, and barrel. Both Betty and Sara were emphatic that they were not leaving their wood cook stoves and both would like to take as much of the furnishings as possible.

Bill went to Sulphur Springs and talked to the carriage maker who had recently moved to Texas from Saint Louis. The man needed to get established and prove his bona fides and was willing to build Bill what he wanted even though freight transportation wagons weren't his main interest. The two wagons were to be loosely patterned after the Conestoga. Bill explained the intended use of the wagons and emphasized they had to be sturdy enough to withstand the rigors of a 1,700 mile trip and carry heavy loads. Bud Robertson, the carriage maker understood and agreed on a price of $280.00 for the two wagons and promised they would be ready by February 10, 1875.

With that out of the way, Bill went to the livery and talked to the hostler about the need to purchase twelve strong farm horses to pull three wagons on a long trip. Bill said he was willing to pay $1,500.00 for the three teams including two sets of harness. Bill looked at the hostler and said, "I don't want any crow bait; these must be healthy specimens. I'm willing to pay top dollar, but I want only the best twelve work horses in Hopkins County." The hostler said for Bill to come back in one week and he would have the horses ready for his inspection.

Bill then went by the newspaper and asked them to run an ad saying that he and Bud were selling the 400 acre ranch and it would be available around the 1st of March. The newspaper man said, "I hate to cost myself a printing job, but there is a man at the hotel right now that wants to buy a ranch. Bud walked down the street to the Sulphur Springs Hotel and asked the clerk to see the man who was in the market to buy a ranch. The clerk said, "You must mean Count Philip."

Bill looked at the clerk and nodded, "That's probably him."

In a few minutes, a man dressed in fancy clothes appeared and introduced himself as Count Philip Gustoff von Huber. Bill shook the man's hand and introduced himself. The Count knew about the Slant BB ranch and was interested. They walked into the dining room for coffee and started discussing price. After they haggled for a time, the Count said, "I would be willing to pay you $5.00 per acre and $300.00 for existing improvements. That would be $2,300.00 if my arithmetic is correct."

Bill shook the Count's hand and said, "Have the funds ready in a week, and Bud and I will be here to sign the papers." That concluded his business in Sulphur Springs, so he returned to the ranch and gave the group the news. In one afternoon, the ranch was sold, and they had the promise of twelve work horses and two cargo wagons. They had the farm wagon which they would convert to a chuck wagon. Since Kaede wasn't going with them, they would need a cook. Betty and Sara would have their hands full managing a brood of kids and driving the two wagons.

Bud had a mischievous grin on his face and said, "I might have a lead on a cook for the trail, and if things work out, this individual might just want to stay on in Montana." The next day, Bud left early in the morning driving the carriage going to Tarrant, Texas, to check on a cook he had heard about. About an hour before dark Bud drove into the yard with a mulatto woman who appeared to be about twenty years old. Bud introduced her as Dorothea Brown, and everyone smiled and shook hands with her. All except Wil, who stood off to the side, changing feet and wringing his hands. Dorothea was tall, perhaps 5' 8," with light brown skin, hair that was dark brown, and dark eyes. She was a very pretty woman.

Dorothea explained that her mother had been a slave on a plantation in Mississippi, which was owned by a man named Samuel Brown. Mr. Brown got her mother pregnant, and Dorothea was the product of the union. When war broke out in Mississippi, Brown brought his slaves to Texas. Dorothea's mother died the third year in Texas from influenza. When the war ended, Dorothea was freed and taken in by a Methodist minister and his wife and raised by them. Dorothea had gotten a job washing dishes in the Tarrant Café and then became the main cook. When the Reverend left to go back east, Dorothea decided to stay in Texas. So here she was with no ties, no family, and no reason not to go to Montana.

Bill, Bud, and Wil worked to separate the cattle for market from the breeding stock all the next week. Mid-morning on a Tuesday, Honks Pickens trotted his horse up to the corral and said, "I understand you pilgrims need an ole cattleman again to keep your fat out of the fire on a drive to Montana."

The next day, Fester Johnson and Josh Ramsey showed up at the ranch. Fester said, "Since I threw in with you folks on the drive to Dodge City, seems I don't have any friends around here. I guess I will eat trail dust for you." With the addition of Pickens, Ramsey, and Johnson, there were now six adult men to make the drive. That was slim on drovers until they got to Kansas and sold the market stock, but they would be fine after that part of the trip was concluded, presuming of course, they got both herds to Kansas.

Bill and Bud were getting ready to go to Tarrant to inspect the work horses when a man rode up followed by two large shaggy dogs. When he stopped, Bud asked him to step down and come in for a cup of coffee. The man introduced himself as Ralph Emery and said that he had a small sheep ranch over by Sulphur Springs. The kids all burst out of the cabins and started hugging the dogs and playing with them. Emery said that he was selling his sheep and going to California to try his hand at finding gold and wanted to sell his dogs. Emery allowed that Duke and Daisy would do the work of four drovers and, other than the initial cost, wouldn't cost a dime. They would eat food scraps and forage for rodents. Bill asked Emery what he had in mind for a price for the two Old English Sheepdogs. Emery said they were worth a lot of money, but there was no market for the animals at the present time. Would Bill and Bud consider $50.00 for the two? Bill pulled out some bills and gave Emery the money.

The dogs were peculiar looking with long shaggy hair that partially covered their faces and eyes. Duke probably weighed around ninety pounds and Daisy about seventy-five. If Emery was telling the truth, they now had nine hands for the trail drive. If not, the two dogs would be great companions for the children and maybe keep them out of Sara and Betty's hair.

Chapter 21

Betty, Dorothea, and Sara got their heads together and made a list of food supplies they would need for the trip. The first leg of the trip to Dodge City, Kansas, was a little more than 500 miles and would take about two months, give or take. There were some way stations on the Chisholm Trail, but what they might have on hand at any given time was a complete unknown.

They decided to buy: twenty pounds of lard, twenty pounds of sugar, ten pounds of rice, two barrels of flour, fifteen pounds of coffee, ten pounds of dried apples, one hundred pounds of beans, fifty pounds of cured bacon, five pounds of salt, two pounds of saleratus (baking powder), two bushels of corn meal, and 100 pounds of pilot bread (hardtack). There was always an ample supply of jerked beef on hand, so they would just pack all they had. In addition to hauling the food supplies, the farm wagon which Bud and Honks had converted into a chuck wagon of sorts would have to haul the Dutch oven, bedrolls for the drovers, farrier supplies, spare firearms, and tenting.

The second wagon would carry and house the seven children, the oldest of which would be seven in May, spare clothes, and serve as the sleeping accommodation for as many people as could be packed in with the kids during bad weather.

The third wagon would haul the wood cook stoves for the new homes, as many furnishings as could be packed into the wagon, and the axes and woodworking tools needed for building new cabins. All three wagons would carry two water barrels.

Bill and Bud rode to Mount Pleasant and met Count von Huber, signed the papers deeding the ranch to him, and received $2,300.00 in U.S. currency. They thanked him and went to the livery to see about the work horses. When they arrived, the hostler brought out thirteen plow horses that all seemed fit and strong. The hostler said, "There are thirteen because I thought you might want a spare in case one got injured or came up lame. One of the homesteaders who are pulling out had three horses. We can do the thirteen horses for $1,600.00 if that is agreeable with you." Bill hadn't thought about a spare, but it wasn't a bad idea and agreed to the price. The hostler agreed to feed, water, and stable the horses until the wagons were ready for $1.25 a day.

Next, they went to the carriage maker to check on the progress and found the man was ahead of schedule. He allowed that if he didn't have problems with the wheels, the wagons would be ready the following week.

Wil would be the horse wrangler for the drive and take care of the thirteen plow horses and the eighteen saddle horses. He would have his hands full. Betty, Dorothea, and Sara would drive the wagons in front of the two herds and attend to the two milk cows. Wil would follow with the remuda. The market herd which was to be sold would come next and was separated from the stock herd for the new ranch by about one-quarter mile. The logic of the market herd being ahead of the breeding herd was so they could feed on the most plentiful grass and add weight before arriving at market. Once the market herd was sold, the breeding herd would have about 1,000 miles to eat all the grass they could find.

On the morning of February 17, 1875, the trail drive started, and Dorothea pulled out headed north in the lead wagon, the entire procession following behind. It would be Dorothea's responsibility to find a camp site and have the evening meal ready when the herd caught up with her. The goal was to cover ten to twelve miles each day.

When the drovers arrived with the first herd, Dorothea had the meal of beans that she had soaked all day in water and a bit of baking powder and then cooked with some chilies and bacon grease, biscuits, and three apple pies ready for the hungry men. The kids had already been fed and were playing around the wagons. Bill walked up and talked to Dorothea for a minute and explained that she had gone a little farther than needed. Ten to twelve miles each day was about the pace he wanted to try to keep, "I figure we went closer to fifteen today."

Dorothea smiled and said, "Cooking is something I'm good at, figuring distance is something I have never done. I will try to do better."

After assigning night herd duties, Bill had a cup of coffee with Bud, visited with Betty and the kids, stretched out below the wagon, placed his head on his saddle, and was immediately asleep.

The drive went well until they got to the Salt Fork Red River. The spring rains had swollen the

Red, and it was high to say the least, not out of the banks, but full to the brim. Bill and Bud had a decision to make, they could swim the cattle across without any real problem at the normal ford but getting the three wagons across was another matter. The bigger concern was the seven small children. If they lost control of the wagon with the kids inside, they might all drown. To compound the problem, there was little grass on which the cattle could graze on the Texas side of the stream. Staying for any extended period of time without grass, waiting for the water level to recede was not a possibility.

Bud came up with the idea of cutting two trees and tying one of them on either side of a wagon with ropes and then placing three men on either side as the wagon crossed the river. The three men riding upstream each had a rope tied to the wagon and around their saddle pommel. They decided to split the children into three groups of two, two, and three. That way if a wagon capsized, the three cowboys on the downriver side could hopefully grab the children and take them across on horseback. They got the chuck wagon ready first and put BJ and Nathan in the seat next to Dorothea and started across the river. There were spots where the wagon wheels got off the bottom and the wagon listed a little, but the crossing went well.

When Dorothea got on the Indian Territory side of the river, she stopped for them to get the logs off the wagon, kept on going for about a mile, and started fixing the evening meal. BJ and Nathan helped by gathering dead wood for the cook fire.

About the time she had supper finished, beans again, the first of the drovers started showing up with the market cattle. Around sunset, everyone had eaten, and the night watch duties had been assigned. Bill, Bud, and Honks discussed their progress and Honks allowed that everything had gone as planned so far, and the wagons had crossed the Red without incident. So far, they had been lucky.

They were now twenty-six days into the drive and had suffered no major problems. They would be in Indian Territory (Oklahoma) for about fifty days where Comancheros, Comanche, and Apache who strayed from the reservations were a possibility. All the Oklahoma Territory Indians were supposedly pacified and on reservations, but hostiles had the tendency to wander off the reservations and cause mischief. Once they crossed into Kansas there would be rustlers who would want to cut the herd. The real trials of the drive were just now beginning.

Chapter 22

The Red River War was the last major conflict between the U.S. Army and the southern Plains Indians. The Medicine Lodge Treaty of 1867 had caused the Southern Cheyenne, Arapaho, Comanche, and Kiowa to move onto reservations in the Indian Territory. Most of the Indians accepted reservation life. Some continued to raid and then returned to the reservations as a sanctuary. Kiowa leaders Satanta and Big Tree were imprisoned in 1872, along with 124 Comanche women and children for a raid they conducted in 1871. The prisoners were released in 1873 and went back to raiding white settlers in Texas, Kansas, Colorado, and Indian Territory.

In 1874, full-scale war broke out on the frontier. Retribution for braves lost in earlier raids, delays and shortages in rations on the reservations, and the loss of their culture due to white men taking over traditional Indian lands caused growing anger amongst the Indians. On June 27, 1874, a group of Comanche attacked a small number of buffalo hunters at Adobe Walls, a small settlement in Hutchinson County, Texas. The attack caused the official beginning of the Red River War. As many as 5,000 Indians, made up of the southern tribes, fled the Indian Territory reservations. The Indian Bureau declared the Indians who had left the reservations as "hostiles." During the spring of 1875, small bands of Kwahadi Comanche, led by Mow-way and Quanah Parker were still roaming western Indian Territory,

North Texas, and Kansas. They would continue to wreak havoc until they finally went to Fort Sill and surrendered on June 2, 1875.

****

Dorothea was driving the chuck wagon and saw three riders approaching from the north. When they got fairly close, it was obvious they were drovers, and they pulled up at her wagon. The older of the three men took off his hat and said, "Morning, Ma'am. Don't mean to scare you, but Geronimo and some of his followers have escaped from the San Carlos Reservation and are roaming around killing and stealing. They would love to have the supplies in your chuck wagon. We haven't seen any Indians, but that doesn't mean they aren't around. If you want to stop, I will leave my two friends with you and go and tell the trail boss the situation."

Dorothea thanked the man for his kindness and said that would be fine. With a Paterson under her apron, she felt safe with the cowboys, and having them with her wouldn't hurt if Indians showed up.

The man, Justin Bickerstaff, passed the two wagons and remuda and found Bud in front of the market herd, explained that he and two other drovers were returning from a trail drive, and gave him the news he had shared with Dorothea. Bickerstaff went on to say that the Comanche were also roaming North Texas and the Indian Territory and had burned out a couple settlers, scalped them, and raped and killed the women. He had neglected to share the last bit of information with Dorothea. Bud thanked Bickerstaff and asked him to ride back to the Montana herd where he could relay the information to Bill.

After listening to Bickerstaff, Bill immediately asked, "Would you and the two other drovers consider working the drive as far as Dodge City? I will pay you $30.00 for a little more than one month's work. An extra three guns will provide a little more security."

Bickerstaff could only speak for himself, but he said he would be glad to join the drive. When they caught up with Dorothea and the other two drovers, the other two men agreed to work the remainder of the drive. One was named Monte Pike and the other Elmer Gilbert. The three cowboys put their slickers and bedrolls into the chuck wagon and asked where Bill wanted them to ride. Bill thought a minute, looked at Bud and Honks, and said, "I think if we get hit by Indians, they will try to cut some steers out of the back herd. It would be easier for them to sneak up and get away from behind." Bud and Honks nodded in agreement. Bill rode off to check with Betty and see how she and the kids were doing.

Bud looked at Bickerstaff and said, "You and Pike stay with the trailing Montana herd, and Gilbert, you go with Honks and stay with the Kansas sale herd."

The new arrangement of the wagons staying close to the lead herd was making for some cold or hastily prepared suppers, but it was necessary to ensure that Dorothea, Betty, Sara, and the children were safe, or as safe as possible.

Two days after the three drovers signed on, they proved their worth. Bill, Bud, and Honks had talked it over and decided to put two drovers with the trail herd and one with the lead herd during the night hours. Shifts would change every three hours. Bill and Bud would pull their shifts to make the work come out even. This immediately earned the respect of the six drovers. It was no big deal to Wil as he had seen them pull more than their share of the load for years.

Bill and Fester Johnson were changing shifts around 3 AM, when they heard a gunshot from the trail herd. They headed their horses in that direction at a gallop. There was enough moonlight to let them see a man on the ground and another man was firing at three or four horsemen. Bill pulled up by the downed man, dismounted, and checked on him. It was Gilbert, and he had a bullet in his upper leg. Bill pulled the bandana from around Gilbert's neck and tied it around his leg above the wound, told him to stay still and keep pressure on the wound, remounted, and rode off toward the firing.

Bill pulled his rifle, took aim and shot a rider out of the saddle. The other three riders turned and rode away. Bill pushed through the milling cattle with his horse, soothing them as he rode, and came out on the other side of the herd. There was a very dead Apache lying on the ground. Bill crossed the herd again, helped Gilbert onto the saddle, and asked

Fester to stay with Pike until morning. He then led Gilbert's horse into camp.

Wil came over and helped Gilbert off his horse, laid him on the ground, took the saddle off his horse, put it under his head for a pillow, and started examining the wound. Wil looked at Gilbert and said, "That bullet has to come out, or you might lose your leg."

Bill was obviously concerned and said, "There isn't a doctor within 100 miles of here in any direction, so how are we going to get the bullet out?"

Wil said, "Well, Captain Brubaker, if Gilbert will allow it, I will try to get it out."

Gilbert looked at Wil with stark fear in his eyes and said, "No offense Mister, but I don't think you are the person I want cutting and digging on my leg."

"None taken, Mr. Gilbert. My master in Mississippi was a doctor, and from time to time, he would have me assist him. I saw him remove several bullets. Shall I get my tools and give it a try?"

Gilbert had tears in his eyes and said, "Guess I don't have much choice. This doctor, how many of his patients lived?"

Wil laughed and said, "A few." Wil went to the chuck wagon, got a small bag, and rolled it open on the ground, took out a scalpel, probe, retractor, and forceps, went to the fire, and sterilized them over the coals.

Bill looked at Wil and said, "Where did you get the medical kit?"

"I asked Bud to order the kit for me, and he picked it up on one of his trips to Mount Pleasant. I think he thought I wanted the tools for the horses to lance boils and remove thorns and such. I figured sooner or later someone was going to catch a piece of lead, and I wanted to be ready."

Wil called for a bottle of rye, rinsed the wound, gave Gilbert a long pull, and then took one himself. Wil took the bandana off Gilbert's leg, wadded it, and said, "You might want to bite on this; I don't have tools to pull broken teeth." With that, Wil asked Bill, Betty, and Sara to help hold Gilbert still. He asked Dorothea to hold the lantern close by so that he could see and lanced the bullet entrance area, dug around with the probe until he located the piece of lead, took the retractor, inserted it and spread the opening, withdrew the probe, inserted the forceps, and pulled out an intact piece of lead. He then asked Gilbert how he was doing, gave him the bullet, took another swig of the rye, and began sewing the incision together. Dorothea looked at Wil like he was Moses and had just parted the Red Sea. To say she was smitten would be a gross understatement.

Bill, Bud, and Honks discussed the Indian problem and decided since there was a three-quarter moon they should move the cattle at night and allow them to graze during the day. It was harder to hit a moving herd, and the cattle could use the extra grazing to fatten up. They used this plan for the remainder of the first part of the drive and arrived at Dodge City without further Indian incidents.

Bill and Bud went into Dodge City and found a man named Jonathan Shorts who was a cattle buyer, who followed them to the herd and said, "I will give you $8.37 a head for these cattle."

Bill said, "Make it $8.50 a head for the lot, and I won't even get a second price."

Shorts said, "Done. I will get a tally, and how do you want to be paid?"

Bill responded, "We would like $5,000.00 wired to our bank, and the rest in greenbacks or gold to pay off drovers and buy supplies for the trip to Montana."

When Bill got back to the camp, Honks came walking up and said, "Captain, I'm not trying to mind your business, but you might want to think about holding out maybe a half-dozen steers to bargain with if we meet up with Indians. Better to give away two or three steers than get in a battle with starving Indians." Bill agreed it was a good idea and told Honks to go ahead and cut six of the most haggard steers out of the herd and move them up with the breeder stock.

The next day, Shorts was at the stock yards and did the tally as the cattle were run into the chute going into the holding corral. He and Bud both did a count as the cattle came through. Both came up with 879 which came to $7,471.50. Bill had the $5,000.00 bank draft wired to the Texas State Bank in Dallas, Texas. Bill and Bud now had $28,000.00 in the bank and cash for expenses for the rest of the trip to Montana. Adjusted for price levels, $28,000.00 in 1870s funds would be worth about $616,000.00

today. They were wealthy cattlemen. Not rich like John Chisum, and certainly not in the league with Cornelius Vanderbilt or Alexander Stewart, but they had exceeded their wildest dreams.

Chapter 23

After getting their trail drive pay, Bickerstaff, Pike, and Gilbert said they were going to the Dodge House for a rye whiskey. Honks Pickens and Wil Byrd had business to attend to in Dodge City. Honks needed to wire some money back to Texas and Wil was going to see the farrier to purchase the parts and pieces he needed for shoeing the horses. The three drovers invited Honks and Wil to have a parting drink with them, so they went along with the three men to the saloon.

When they had ordered their drinks, a fancy dressed man with two pearl handled .45s in matching holsters hollered across the room, "Hey, you, the buck ape, get out of the saloon. There will be no Niggers, Mexicans, or Indians in here." Wil ignored the man and took a sip of his drink.

The gunfighter walked over to the bar about ten feet from Wil and said, "Nigger, are you deaf? I said get out." Bickerstaff, Pike, Gilbert, and other men started backing away from the bar until all that were left was Honks, Wil, and the gunfighter.

Wil slowly turned and faced the gunfighter and said, "I don't carry a pistol; never had any use for one."

The gunfighter, who they later learned was named Wiley Smith, smiled an evil smirk and said, "That's not a problem; I'll loan you one." He then pulled one of his pistols out of its holster, laid it on the bar, and slid it down behind Wil.

Honks glanced at Smith and said, "Don't push this, son."

"I ain't your son, you ole geezer, and this ain't your fight."

Honks turned slightly to face Smith and said, "Young fella, I know you aren't my son. I couldn't have sired a polecat like you. Wil told you he don't use a pistol. Killing him would be murder. But, I have used mine from time to time. If you are so all hell fired anxious to leave this world, I will see you measured and read over."

The gunfighter laughed and responded, "That's mighty bold talk for an ole worn out cowboy."

The barkeep spoke up and said, "I wouldn't brace Smith, mister. He has killed a dozen men in gunfights."

Honks glanced at the barkeep and replied, "Any reason to believe he shot any of them from the front?" He then looked at Smith and said, "Last chance to walk away, son. By the way, only fairies and fops carry pearl handle pistols. Which are you?"

Smith bristled and went for his gun. Honks didn't look fast, just one continuous fluid motion as he drew his Colt Dragoon revolver and fired. The bullet hit Smith just to the left of his watch pocket. Smith looked surprised for a couple moments, kneeled down, and fell to the floor. Honks holstered his pistol and turned back to his beer as if nothing had happened. The three drovers came back to the bar and just shook their heads in disbelief. Cowboys, especially old ones, were not supposed to be all that good with a gun.

Honks and Wil waited until the town marshal came to the saloon and asked members of the crowd what had happened. Each told basically the same story: Smith had pushed the fight, drew first, and got what he deserved. The marshal told Honks he was free to go, and he and Wil left the saloon. Honks and Wil went to the Western Union telegraph office, and Pickens wired $100.00 to his bank account in Mount Pleasant, Texas. They then went to the farrier's shop and purchased the things Wil would need to keep the horses' hooves in good repair.

****

New York & Western Union Telegraph Company and the New York and Mississippi Valley Printing Telegraph Company were competitors for all the telegraph business in the growing United States. They consolidated their companies and named the new company Western Union. In 1861, it opened the first transcontinental telegraph service. Western Union introduced the first stock ticker in 1866. In 1871, Western Union introduced its money transfer service which used its extensive telegraph network. From the time Honks walked into the telegraph office in Dodge City, Kansas, to the time the money was received in the bank in Mount Pleasant, Texas, only a few minutes had passed. Once the money was logged into Honks' account, it was ready for withdrawal.

****

When they got back to the camp Honks let Bill and Bud know that he was back. He thought it best to let his bosses know about the shooting and gave them an abbreviated version of the confrontation. After filling them in, Honks went to the fire and got a cup of coffee. Bill looked at Bud, shook his head, and said, "Did you notice that Honks told us about killing a man just like he would if it were a snake? I think there is a lot in his past that we don't know and maybe don't want to know."

Wil went to the chuck wagon, using the excuse of getting a cup of coffee, to talk to Dorothea. Bill and Bud mounted their horses and rode off to check the herd. As Wil was sitting cross-legged and trying to impress Dorothea, one of the children screamed, "Scorpion." Wil dropped his cup, got up, and ran to the little boys who had been gathering wood. BJ, Nathan, and William would gather small limbs and such for firewood whenever the wagons stopped for the day. Bill and Bud had cautioned them to be careful about snakes, Gila monsters, and scorpions. They could be hard to see as their coloring blended in with whatever they were near. It seems everything in the west stung, bit, or otherwise pierced the skin.

When Wil got to the boys, he saw a large striped bark scorpion, about three inches long, and stomped it with his boot. BJ said, "It bit Nathan on the hand." Wil sat Nathan down and looked at his hand. It was already beginning to swell. About that time Sara ran up and went hysterical. Wil turned to Sara and said, "Miss Sara, you must get ahold of yourself; I have to treat this child." Lancing the wound would have no effect, so Wil picked Nathan up and carried him to the wagons. He placed the child in the back of the empty wagon, and Sara took the little boy in her arms and sobbed. Wil went to his saddle bags and got a plug of chewing tobacco, took a chaw, wallered it around his mouth for a couple minutes until it was a juicy mess, and then placed it on the site of the scorpion bite and wrapped it with a cloth.

Wil walked back to where Nathan had been bitten and looked for other scorpions but saw none. He walked back to the wagon and told Sara, "I didn't mean to speak harsh to you, but I needed to work fast before the boy went into shock. I think the boy will be fine, but he is going to be mighty sick for a couple days. Make sure he drinks lots of water to help flush out any poison that may have gotten in his body. Through sobs Sara put her hand on Wil's arm and said, "Think nothing of it; I understand. Thanks for what you did for Nathan."

BJ had **gone** and told his Pa about Nathan being bit by the scorpion and Bud put the boy behind the saddle, mounted, and came **on the run**. Wil got him calmed down and said, "Bud, I think Nathan will be fine, just sick for a couple days. It might be a good idea to wait it out here before we move the herd to make sure." They stayed two days, and Sara never left the child's side other than to take care of bodily functions. Nathan had fever, chills, was delirious at times, and the hand swelled up. To make matters worse, the boy vomited and had trouble keeping water in his stomach. The first day and night were touch and go. The fever broke on the afternoon of the second day. On the third day after the bite, Nathan wanted to get up and play but sure had a sore hand. Without Wil's swift action to stabilize and reassure the boy, he could have gone into shock and died. Nathan was a very lucky little boy.

****

The bite of the striped bark scorpion, *C. vittatus* is rarely lethal. The sting is extremely painful and causes localized swelling to the site of the bite. The neurotoxins in the venom are known to cause muscle spasms, nausea and vomiting, shortness of breath, and in some cases, anaphylactic shock. The venom of the *C. vittatus* contains several different proteins, each of which can cause a different reaction in the human body.

****

While waiting for Nathan's body to overcome the scorpion venom, Bill got two extra horses from the remuda, put panniers on one, a saddle on the other, and took Dorothea along with him to Dodge City to select supplies for the chuck wagon. Dorothea went into the emporium, and Bill went to the harness shop. It seemed the entire town was abuzz regarding the old cowboy who had killed the gunfighter. The harness maker said he had been in the saloon when the older man had killed the gunfighter and had never seen anything like it. The old cowboy just pulled his pistol, shot the gunfighter, holstered his pistol, and turned back to his drink like nothing had happened.

Honks hadn't elaborated on the shooting or said a word about the specifics of the incident. An older man who could kill a gunfighter and think nothing of it wasn't a man to mess with. Honks Pickens was easy going, and Bill had never seen him angry. Now he hoped he never did. After getting the harness repaired, Bill went and paid for the goods Dorothea had ordered. Bill asked the clerk what school books he had, and the man said, "I have Watson and McGuffy readers from first through fifth grade, the Complete Arithmetic Book, A Geography for Beginners, and A Pictorial History of the United States." Bill purchased what the store owner had on hand and had them wrapped in one large bundle. When they got back to the camp and Bill showed the school books to Sara, she was thrilled. She didn't want the children to grow up ignorant and was going to start their lessons at age five, and BJ, Mattie, and Nathan were ready to start.

After it was obvious Nathan was going to be all right, Dorothea, Betty, and Sara started out with the wagons at a leisurely pace right after breakfast and stayed within sight of the herd. They had almost 800 miles in front of them before they would be in Montana, so there was no reason to hurry.

Chapter 24

The second leg of the long trip to Montana started in Dodge City, Kansas, with the first layover scheduled for Fort Wallace, Kansas, which was about 150 miles. Then from Fort Wallace, Kansas, to Denver, Colorado, would be about 200 miles. Then from Denver, Colorado, to Fort Collins, Colorado, which was another sixty-five miles. Then from Fort Collins, Colorado, to Fort D. A. Russell, Wyoming, which was only forty-five miles. Then from Fort D. A. Russell, Wyoming, to Fort Fetterman, Wyoming, which was another 140 miles. From Fort Fetterman, Wyoming, to the Little Missouri River in Montana which was about another 200 miles. All totaled, they would travel 800 miles, give or take. The layovers were planned to be at military forts in order to rest, resupply, make repairs, and get information on possible hostile activity. There were three trails which led to the northwest: Old Military Trail, Omaha Trail, and Smokey Hill Trail. The Slant BB would use portions of all three before arriving at their destination in Montana.

****

The Old Military Trail connected Fort Wallace, near Eagle Tail Station, Kansas, to Fort Lyon, near Las Animas, Colorado, on the Arkansas River. The Omaha Trail led out of Kansas into Wyoming at Fort D. A. Russell near the South Platte River in Laramie County. It then merged with the

Smoky Hill Trail east of Cheyenne Wells, Colorado. The Smoky Hill Trail was also called the Butterfield Trail. It followed the Smoky Hill River and was promoted as the most direct route to Denver, Colorado, for those traveling to the Nebraska and Kansas Territories. Several army forts were established along the trail to protect travelers. The trail split near "Old Wells," near present day Cheyenne Wells, Colorado, into north and south forks. The north fork went northwest through Deering Wells Station, Big Springs Station, David Wells Station, and then to Denver, Colorado. The south fork ran southwest from Old Wells through Eureka Station to Dubois Station. Then it headed northwest to Grady Station. The two forks joined up again near Hugo, Colorado.

****

When the Slant BB group and their mixed breed cattle herd left Dodge City, Kansas, they were entering another world, filled with danger and challenges, not the least of which were the Indians who roamed the Great Plains. When the group left Dodge City, Kansas, there were seven men, three women, and seven young children. Two dogs and two milk cows rounded out the group. Bill had ordered new Colt Model 73 .45 revolvers from Rufus Maxwell's store in the 5 and 1/2 inch barrels, and gotten ten: two each for him and Bud, one each for Sara and Betty and four as spares and for the boys as they got older. Bill ordered 1,000 rounds of .45 pistol cartridges, six boxes of 10 gauge buckshot, and 1,000 rounds of .44 rim fire cartridges for the Henry rifles. Then 500 rounds of large bore ammunition for the Sharps carbines. Bill had also ordered six of the new 1873 Winchester level action rifles in .44-40 caliber along with 1,000 rounds of ammunition for them and traded the old Spencer rifles in against the bill.

The Slant BB crew was better armed than the army on the frontier, but there were still only ten adults to shoot the weapons. Bud had been working with Wil to get him to influence Dorothea to learn to shoot. When Wil had first come to the ranch, he had been reluctant to fire a gun. Slaves were not allowed to own or shoot firearms, and that was still ingrained in him. Wil had overcome that fear some time back and through practice had become a crack shot with a rifle but had no interest in a pistol. Bud was finding it a challenge to teach Dorothea to shoot. At first, she had no interest in weapons, and then Bud had a chat with her. Bud looked sternly and said, "Dorothea, if Indians get past the men, they will rape you, Betty, and Sara until you are dead; then they will either kill the children or take them to be raised as Indians. Every adult on this drive has to be able to pull their weight. That includes helping to defend our lives and property if necessary." After that conversation Dorothea, saw the wisdom in learning to use a rifle and the Paterson pistol and became a fairly proficient marksman or markswoman as it were.

Mattie Lea was seven, and BJ had just turned five, a little young to fire the big rifles, but old enough to load them which became their job. Bud brought out the Henry and Winchester rifles, laid them out on the end of the wagon for Mattie Lea and BJ to examine, and showed them how to insert the cartridges in each weapon. He then had them load the Winchesters and eject the shells, and had them do it again, and again, and again, until he was confident they could do their job if the need arose. He then went through the same drill with the Henry rifles. Children on the frontier had toys and their play time, but at an early age, they were entrusted with duties and responsibilities.

On the second day of the leg of the drive to Fort Wallace, Kansas, Dusty and Fester were with the cattle while everyone else was sitting around the campfire, the men drinking coffee, the women talking about the next day's activities, dresses, and the homes they were going to have in Montana. The children were sitting and listening to the conversations. All of a sudden, Nathan, Bud's son who had inherited his father's gift of gab, blurted out, "I saw Mister Wil and Miss Dorothea kissing beside the wagon last night." Everyone turned and looked at the child, then at Wil and Dorothea who both wanted to disappear. Bud broke the tension by laughing, and then everyone joined in.

Wil looked at Bill and said, "Captain, would you go into Fort Wallace when we camp near the fort and see if the army chaplain will marry Dorothea and me?"

Bill smiled and replied, "Well, if the two of you are going to continue upsetting the children by kissing, I suppose I had better do that." Bud and the rest of the crew joined in on the joke. Wil and Dorothea didn't see the humor.

Honks spoke up and said, "By jiminy, if I had known you were going to lose your freedom again, I might have let that gunfighter shoot you." The joking concluded, the men all shook hands with Wil and Sara and Betty hugged Dorothea.

When they neared Fort Wallace, they set up camp, rested the cattle, and allowed them to graze on the tall grass about two miles away from the fort. Bill rode to the fort and asked to speak to the post chaplain. The fort commander said they didn't have a chaplain at the present time because he had been called to duty at another post and his replacement had yet to arrive. Bill told the commander there was a man and woman on the trail drive who wanted to get hitched. The commander thought a moment and said, "I think I have the authority as the fort commander to perform that function. When do you want to do this?"

Bill said, "Other than buying supplies, filling our water barrels from the Smoky Hill River, and seeing if your wheelwright can do a repair or two on one of the wagon wheels, we should be ready to leave the day after tomorrow."

The young Captain said, "Why don't we plan on tomorrow evening just before sunset. I will come out to your camp if that is all right." The plans being made, Bill went to the wheelwright shop and gained permission to bring a cracked wheel in for repair. He rode back to the camp and gave Wil and Dorothea the news. He then got Dusty and Fester to help lift the wagon, using a pole for a lever so the wheel could be removed, and stacked rocks under the axle. Wil found two small pine trees and cut them down and built a travois to haul the wheel to the fort and back.

Sara and Betty had fixed a nice dinner, and Dorothea was outfitted in her best dress when the fort commander arrived. Wil had gone to the Smoky Hill River, bathed, and beat all the trail dust he could from his clothes. When the fort commander saw he was about to marry Negroes, he blanched but didn't say anything. After performing the ceremony, Bill and Bud thanked him and invited him to stay and eat with them. He declined saying he needed to get back to the fort. The Captain gave Wil and Dorothea a signed paper stating they were married and the date.

After dinner and a few drinks to celebrate, Wil and Dorothea excused themselves and walked off into the darkness with a blanket. Nathan, always the inquisitive one said, "Where are Wil and Miss Dorothea going?"

Bill never missed a beat and said, "To check on the cattle. They may be gone a while."

Bud sat in silence for a few moments and then said, "Looks like I have three cabins to build when we get to Montana. I should have stayed in Missouri and gone into the carpentry business. Everyone laughed. It was to be the last enjoyable night for some time.

The next morning Bill and Fester rode to the fort, secured the repaired wheel on the travois, mounted it on the wagon, and the journey continued.

Chapter 25

Following the end of the Civil War, all American Indians were assigned to reservations. The job of the army was to keep them there. One of the problems was that not all the Indians went to the reservations and many who did had no intention of staying, escaped at the first opportunity, and attempted to return to their native land. Some made it and some were recaptured. The reservations were under the control of the Interior Department. The actual control of the Great Plains fell to the Army's Department of the Missouri which attempted to administer an area of more than 1,000,000 square miles of frontier extending from the Mississippi River to the Rocky Mountains. There weren't enough soldiers or Indian knowledge to effectively perform the job.

During the 1860s and 1870s there were treaties, atrocities on both the Indian and Anglo sides, and numerous skirmishes between the army and the hostiles. In 1875, the U.S. Government stopped evicting trespassers from the Black Hills of the Dakotas and offered to purchase the land. The Sioux refused to sell, and the government gave the Indians until January 31, 1876, to leave the Black Hills and return to the government reservations. The Sioux didn't return, and Lieutenant Colonel George Armstrong Custer was tasked with the unenviable job of forcing them to go back to the reservations. Custer and his 7th Cavalry stumbled upon the main body of the Lakota and other tribes encamped on the

Little Big Horn River in Montana Territory during the late afternoon of June 25, 1876.

Custer advanced ahead of his reinforcements, and without foreknowledge of the number of Indians he faced, he and most of his 7th Cavalry were killed. The U. S. government called it the massacre at the Little Big Horn, and the Indians called it the battle of Greasy Grass. Public sentiment was led by an advertising campaign by the Anheuser-Busch brewery which ordered reprints of the painting "Custer's Last Fight," had them framed and placed in hundreds of saloons. The painting didn't accurately depict the engagement, but it did stir emotions and hatred against the Indians.

Those who have visited the Little Bighorn Battlefield National Monument will have noticed that the grave markers of the individual soldiers don't match the famous painting. Individual grave markers are scattered over the better part of a mile in individual or small groups as the men ran for their lives in the face of the overwhelming number of Indians. Indians who were later interviewed claimed that Colonel Custer was actually the first casualty of the engagement as he was shot while leading a small detachment across the Little Big Horn River. Since Colonel Custer and his younger brother Thomas looked much alike, it could have been the younger Custer who was killed fording the river. Irrespective of the details, there is no disagreement as to whether Custer and all the cavalry members who accompanied him were killed.

The killing of Custer and his men, while a glorious victory for the Plains Indians, also served to seal their doom as free people. The army's retribution was immediate and brutal and forced the majority of the tribes back to reservations.

****

In the spring and summer of 1875 when the Slant BB herd, drovers, and wagons were pressing northwest towards Montana, small bands of Sioux and Cheyenne were raiding mail stagecoaches, burning stage stations, and killing employees. They were also raping, killing, and kidnapping settlers on the frontier. While most of the activity was to the west of the trail used by the Slant BB, there were still small bands of hostiles roaming the countryside.

Two days out of Fort Wallace a small group of rustlers hit the herd in the early morning hours. Bud and Dusty were riding the early morning shift and saw the cattle being led off by three men on horseback. Bud and Dusty didn't fire their weapons for fear of causing the cattle to stampede. Bud rode back to the camp and rousted out Bill and told him what had happened. Bill got Honks up and told him to saddle up, and the two of them would go after the rustlers. Bud asked, "Don't you need some help?"

Bill looked at Bud and said, "Didn't you say there was only three of them? With Honks with me, we will have them outnumbered." Bill saddled a mare from the remuda and put his new Winchester

1873 .44-40 caliber carbine into the scabbard and asked Honks if he wanted one of the new rifles.

Honks said, "I don't ever carry a weapon I haven't proven; I will keep my ole Dragoons and my Winchester 1866 Golden Boy. But thanks anyway. Are we bringing back anything but cattle?"

Bill looked at the camp fire, and when he lifted his eyes there was sadness to them, and he said, "No, just the cattle." With that Honks went to the wagon and got two Ames "T" handle shovels and tied one behind each of their saddles.

Bill and Honks had a couple cups of coffee and then lit out at first light. The rustler's trail wasn't hard to follow, and they caught up with them about mid-day camped next to a copse of trees by a small creek, drinking coffee and laughing. Bill said he would circle well wide to the right and Honks could do the same to the left and they would hopefully approach undetected and have the rustlers in a cross fire, but hopefully they wouldn't have to waste bullets on these critters. Both men stopped at their respective end of the copse of trees, dismounted, tied their horses to trees, and walked as quietly as possible through the forest. When Bill got to within thirty yards of the camp, he hollered out, "You, by the fire, don't move a muscle." With that he walked towards their camp.

From the other side of the camp Honks spoke up and said, "Don't think about going for your guns. We would cut you to rag dolls."

The oldest of the three men spoke up and said, "I don't know what's got you fellas so riled up.

We're just sitting here drinking coffee and were just fixin to take these steers that wandered up to our camp back to their owner."

Bill looked at the man and said, "I was born, but not yesterday. Three men were seen cutting our herd, and we trailed them and these cattle with my brand to your camp. Take out your guns really slow, with just your index finger and thumb, and put them on the ground." When they were disarmed, Bill told Honks to tie the men's hands behind their backs.

The oldest man spoke up and said, "What have you got in mind?"

"I will get no enjoyment out of this, but I am going to do what rustlers earn on the frontier. I'm going to hang all three of you." Honks got the rustlers horses saddled, took their ropes, tied nooses, placed a noose around each of their necks, led each to a water oak beside the creek, threw the ropes over a large limb, and then tied the ropes to each rider's saddle pommel.

Bill asked the rustlers if they had family they wanted him to notify when he got to the next settlement. They all declined. He then asked if they wanted to provide their names for the grave markers. Again they declined. Bill slapped the horses' rumps, and the three men swung in the air with first their bladders and then their bowels releasing.

Hooks said as much to himself as Bill, "Hanging a man is a horrible thing. This ain't my first necktie party, but I hope it is my last. I have lost friends who were stomped to death by cattle stampeded by rustlers, lost friends who were killed by rustlers, lost cattle to rustlers, and spent days trying to round up cattle that were run off by rustlers."

Bill nodded in understanding and said, "We need to cut these men down and dig three graves."

Honks looked at Bill and replied, "Boss, I'll do whatever you want, but since we don't have any names, why not just dig one grave large enough for all three?" Bill thought a few moments and simply said ok. After digging the grave, they rolled the men in it, and Bill read over them. They tied the rustlers' horses' reins together, put the gun belts around the saddle pommels, and Honks led two horses and Bill the third back to camp. The weapons were taken off the horses and placed in the chuck wagon: two Henrys, one Sharps carbine, one Walker Colt which had been converted to metal cartridges, and two Colt Peacemakers. They had no place to store the saddles, so they just left them on the ground and took the horses to Wil to become part of the remuda. There were no brands on the horses, so there was no reason not to keep them. Wil heated a Slant BB branding iron and branded the three horses.

While everyone was eating supper, Bud tried to relieve some of the tension in the air by asking Honks how he came to have his name. Honks said, "When I was a tad, my friends and Pa said that I honked like a goose when I laughed, so everyone just started calling me Honks."

"Honks, what's your Christian name?"

"Honks will do fine."

Bud persisted, "What if you die out here on the prairie? We would need to know your Christian name to put on your maker."

Honks kinda looked off into the night and mumbled, "Alowishus Winfield."

Bud laughed and said, "What did you say?"

Honks replied, "You heard me, dammit. I knew you would make fun of the name."

After the children had been put to bed, Bill addressed the entire group. "I got no satisfaction out of hanging those men. This is a land without law, harsh, and unforgiving. Human compassion is taken as a sign of weakness. You would think as big as this country is no one would know what was going on, but word has a way of traveling from saloon to saloon. If I had let those men go, we would have rustlers hitting us for a few cows here and a few cows there, or maybe a group of rustlers would try to take the entire herd. Either way, we would arrive in Montana with nothing. Let's all get some sleep." Everyone knew his wisdom was correct. Still it was a horrible thing to hang men.

****

In the American West of the 19th century, rustling was considered a serious offense and did frequently result in hanging. On the frontier, peace officers and courts were few and far between. Jack Sully, who was born Arthur McDonald and Ellen Lilly Watson (Cattle Kate), were two of the best known cattle rustlers in the Dakota and Wyoming

Territories in the late 19th century. Sully and his gang were responsible for stealing an estimated 50,000 head of cattle and 3,000 horses and for killing seven people during his rustling days. He was killed by United States Marshall Johnny Petrie in 1904 at the Rosebud Indian Reservation in South Dakota, when he refused to surrender.

The details regarding Ellen Watson are somewhat less cut and dried. She was hanged in 1889 by a group of cattlemen led by a range detective named George Henderson. Ms. Watson was the only woman ever hanged for the supposed crime of cattle rustling. Some contend that she was hanged because she was a successful homesteader who owned water rights needed by ranchers; others contend she was a prostitute and dealt in stolen cattle. Dozens of lesser known rustlers were caught and hanged, while others managed to elude cattlemen and the law.

Chapter 26

On the prairie, one could see for a mile or more in any direction which made it near impossible for rustlers or Indians to sneak up on the Slant BB herd without being detected in time for everyone to get out the weapons and set up a defense. Once the sun went down, it was another story. Indians were supposed to be afraid to attack at night because they thought if they were killed in the darkness their soul would wander for eternity in darkness. Apparently, there was no belief that they shouldn't steal cattle at night.

About ten days out of Denver, Colorado, Honks and Fester were riding the early morning shift with the herd when about ten Indian braves came riding out of the darkness and cut about fifteen cattle out of the herd. Honks pulled his Winchester 1866 and dropped one of the Indians off his horse, fired again, and hit another who leaned across his horse's neck to keep from falling. With a few whoops, the Indians rode off with the cattle.

The camp was awakened by the gun fire. Everyone got up, and the men were getting their horses saddled when Honks rode in. Honks said to no one in particular, "Cheyenne or at least the one I killed was Cheyenne. They cut about fifteen head and rode west."

Bill asked, "How many were there?"

"I took it to be ten. I killed one and put lead in another, so if my count is correct, there are eight remaining that are apt to put up a fight."

Bill looked at Bud and said, "I would like for you to keep the cattle moving and take care of everything. I will take Honks and Fester with me and get our cows back."

"Bill, why not take a couple more men? There are eight Indians left by Honks' estimation who could put up a fight."

"No, Bud, we don't know if there are more Indians in the area. And these could just be trying to draw us away from the herd. I will feel better if you keep the three men with you and keep the women, children, and our cattle and supplies safe." With that, Bill went over to Betty and kissed her, hugged the kids, and headed west with Honks and Fester riding alongside him.

Bill and the men had followed the trail of the cattle and unshod horses for just a few miles when the grassland began transitioning into foothills which would eventually lead to the far distant mountains. The tracks of several cows were easy enough to follow, but what they would encounter when they caught up with the Indians was the unknown. It could be eight or eighty hostiles.

Around mid-afternoon, Bill saw the cows bunched up in a tight group in a large fissure at the end of a box canyon through his binoculars, but no Indians were to be seen. Bill wasn't an experienced Indian fighter by any stretch of the imagination, but he could smell a trap from his Civil War days. He looked at Honks and asked, "What do you think: a trap waiting to be sprung if we ride in to get the cattle?"

Honks thought a few seconds and responded, "I would wager a month's pay that the hostiles are lying in those rocks above the cattle. What worries me is I don't see their horses." The words were no more than out of Honk's mouth when five Indians on horseback came charging from behind the three cowboys, whooping and screaming in an effort to frighten the men. It worked, but only to a degree. All three cowboys already had their rifles out and turned their horses and fired at the approaching Indians. Two went down to the ground, and a third dropped his rifle and was hanging onto his horse's mane for dear life as three Indians galloped off back to wherever they had been hiding.

Just then, there were gun shots from the direction of the cows and Fester tumbled out of his saddle. Bill and Honks quickly dismounted and pulled their horses to the ground and got behind them. Fester was crawling and trying to get behind a fairly large rock when an Indian stood to put another bullet in him. Honks fired, hit the hostile, and the Indian tumbled over the rock he had been hiding behind. If Honks was correct in his initial estimation of ten Indians, there were four left, and only two who would be up for a fight. Five had charged them on horseback, which would leave three behind them, and one of them was wounded. There were four in the rocks. One of them was now dead, and another was either dead or wounded somewhere from Honk's bullet during the attack on the herd.

Fester had made it to the rock and was trying to use his bandana as a compress to stop the bleeding coming from his left shoulder area. Bill hollered, "Fester, are you hit bad?"

"Naw, Captain, I'm hit in the shoulder. Wil is going to have another bullet to dig out. I'll be fine. Do what you have to do."

Bill looked at Honks and said, "Let's see if we can root those three out of the rocks. I will go around to the right; you take the left. Be careful. We don't have a board long enough to put your whole name on." As Bill and Honks started to flank the three Indians in the rocks, the hostiles jumped up and ran, dodging through the rocks, past the cattle, in the direction where the mounted Indians had retreated. Unfortunately for him, one of the Indians who was limping ran right by the rock Fester was using for shelter. As the hostile dashed by, Fester shot him through the side. The bullet must have gone into his heart because the Indian dropped like a log and never moved.

Presuming Honks count was accurate, the Indians number was down to four, and two of them were carrying slugs in their hide. When they heard the Indians riding off, Bill and Honks scurried back to their horses, got Fester on his feet and then on his horse and walked their horses to the cattle. Honks circled the group of cows and moved them out towards the open grassland. They would be just as well off in the open as in the rocks. The longer they waited to move the cattle back towards the herd, the greater the risk that more hostiles might show up. When they cleared the foothills, they could see four horsemen in the distance headed towards the southwest.

Honks said, "We got lucky again. Every one of these scrapes we get in increases the chances of one of us getting to visit an early grave. Sooner or later we, or I, will get the short end of the stick. Considering the Indians I have put in the ground, it would be only fair if they returned the favor."

When they got back to the camp, Wil got out his medical tools again and removed the bullet from Fester's shoulder, bandaged it, and said, "That could have been a lot worse. Must have been an old or small powder charge; the bullet didn't go very deep. You should be riding drag in a couple days."

Bill said, "According to Honks, that was a Northern Cheyenne war party. We have to presume there are more of them around. I know we are all bone tired, but let's double the night guard and be vigilant. As we get closer to Denver, the terrain is going to get rockier and provide lots of hiding places for Indians or rustlers. I don't want to lose any cows, but I sure don't want to lose any men. Keep your eyes peeled."

They arrived outside Denver on May 20, 1875, without further incident and camped on the south bank of the South Platte River. Bud got a list of supplies that were needed for the chuck wagon from Dorothea. He asked Betty and Sara if there was anything he could get for them and both spoke in unison, "A hot bath!"

Bill said, "Let me go on to town and see what's going on. If everything seems peaceful, perhaps Bud and I can take the two of you to Denver for a meal and a hot bath."

Bill went to the general store in Denver and gave the supplies list to the store clerk and told him he would be back the next day with a wagon to pick everything up. He then walked across the street to the Gold Nugget Saloon. He ordered a beer and talked to the barkeep about the Indian situation in the area. The bartender allowed that there were rumors about Sioux to the west of Denver but no word of anything close by. Bill told him about their experience with the Cheyenne and added that they had hung three rustlers about 100 miles back down the trail. He knew the word of both incidents would get around.

Denver was nothing to scream about. There were tents, brothels, filth in the streets, dogs wandering around, and drunks urinating beside buildings. There was a barber shop and a bath house which offered hot baths, but Bill figured he, and Bud would have to guard their wives like they were a gold shipment.

When Bill got back to camp he found Bud, explained the circumstances, and suggested they take the wives to Denver, get the supplies loaded in the wagon while the women were bathing, have a meal at the Denver House, and let the drovers get a day's rest. He got no argument from Bud, who allowed that a hot bath wouldn't be too bad for his own self. They agreed they would leave the next day about noon, load the wives in the wagon, drive the six or so miles into Denver, and get back before dark. Bill warned the wives that Denver wasn't a refined place, and

176

they would have to stay close to their husbands while in the town. There wasn't to be any straying off without Bill and Bud.

Chapter 27

In preparation for their big city outing, Betty and Sara asked Dorothea if she would look after the children while they accompanied their husbands into Denver to buy some necessities, get a hot bath, and eat in a sit down restaurant. Dorothea told them it would be her pleasure to watch the kids and try to make sure they didn't get into any mischief. She asked if they would mind getting her some green or brown wool yarn and a couple wooden knitting needles so she could make Wil a scarf. They told her they were happy to oblige.

Bill and Bud hooked the work horses to the basically empty wagon used to haul clothes and the children and set out for the short ride to Denver. When they arrived, they pulled the wagon up in front of the Colorado Emporium and general store. The women went inside, shopped a mite, got Dorothea's yarn and needles, and got directions to a bathhouse where they could each enjoy a long hot bath. Bill and Bud accompanied their wives to the bathhouse and then went to the barber shop, got a hair trim and shave, and then a bath in a building behind the barbershop. Next, they went to the Rocky Mountain Saloon and had a rye whiskey and talked to the barkeep. The story was fairly much the same as Bill had heard in the Gold Nugget Saloon the day before. All the hostiles were believed to be west of Denver.

There were men who appeared to be drovers in the saloon, and Bud walked over to the table where they were sitting and asked if they knew anything about the trail to Fort Collins. They agreed that it was an easy trail with plenty of grass and water. They offered that they had encountered no trouble on their last drive.

Bill and Bud met Betty and Sara at the bathhouse and escorted them to the emporium. The owner had the stock boy help carry the supplies to the wagon where Bud stacked them in an orderly fashion. After getting everything loaded, the women climbed into the wagon and made themselves comfortable in the back. Bill and Bud took the seat, and they started back to the camp. Bill had been informed that the food in Denver consisted of buffalo meat and beans, and since they were all tired of buffalo hunters gawking at the women and making them uncomfortable, they decided to skip the dinner. Betty and Sara contended that it was the best day in a long time. Sometimes the little comforts are the most important and enjoyable. It was amazing how much a hot bath could do for the soul.

****

The Rocky Mountains stretch from northern British Columbia in Canada some 3,000 miles to New Mexico in the United States. The mountains contain wilderness areas, an abundance of wildlife, alpine lakes, and unimaginable beauty. The Rocky Mountains were formed around eighty million years in the distant past during the Laramide orogeny in which a number of plates began sliding underneath the North American plate. The angle of subduction was shallow, resulting in a broad belt of mountains running down western North America. Since then, tectonic activity and erosion caused by glacier activity sculpted the Rockies into breathtaking peaks and valleys. The Rocky Mountains contain the highest peaks in central North America.

****

The Slant BB headed out from Denver to Fort Collins on May 23, 1875. This part of the journey was the most beautiful of the entire trek to this point. Off to their left were the majestic Rocky Mountains with winter snow still covering the mid to higher elevations. The trail had an abundance of grass and small creeks for the cattle to water. Two days out of Denver, Wil shot a Pronghorn, an interesting animal that looks like an antelope but is neither goat nor antelope and is unique to the western United States. Betty and Sara dressed out the animal, and it made an excellent meal and change of diet for the group that night.

The evenings began to settle into a routine. Mattie and BJ were old enough to start learning their ABCs and reading a little, along with learning their numbers. Dorothea was in charge of cooking the evening meal. Betty cleaned up the utensils, and Sara would begin the school lessons right after the evening meal. Neither Wil nor Dorothea could read or write, and Sara insisted that they sit in on the lessons. Both were intelligent, but slaves had not been allowed to become educated. Betty was self-educated and had learned to read and write with Bill's help.

The days of tranquility of the drive didn't last long. The next afternoon, Dorothea, in the lead, stopped the chuck wagon near the North Platte River and decided to take a bath before starting supper for the crew. After she came out of the river and put her clothes back on, two buffalo hunters were sitting on their horses grinning at her. One jumped off his horse and grabbed her by the arm and got a handful of fingernails across the nose as Dorothea screamed. The man backhanded Dorothea and heaved her up to the second man, and both men headed out along the river.

Sara heard the scream and grabbed her rifle but didn't dare shoot because of fear of hitting Dorothea. She screamed at Betty to watch the children and ran all the way to the remuda and told Wil what had happened. Wil pulled his lasso and flipped it around a roan gelding, took the saddle off his tired horse, saddled the roan, took his rifle out of the scabbard, and said, "Tell Captain Brubaker I will be back as soon as I recover Dorothea." With that, he rode off toward the river at a gallop, picked up the trail of the two horses, and lit out after them.

After a couple miles, Wil came to a slight rise and stopped. Below him among a small copse of trees were the two buffalo hunters and Dorothea. One of the men was pawing at Dorothea's dress, and as he ripped it off, he stood back a mite and started unbuttoning his britches. Wil took aim and fired his rifle. The bullet caught the man slightly higher than Wil aimed and entered the man's face from the side just below his nose and literally blew off his face. Wil levered in another shell as the second man went for his Sharps .50 caliber buffalo gun. Wil snap-shot the buffalo hunter in the gut, and the man just sat down on the ground and dropped the rifle.

Wil led his horse down to the trees and hugged Dorothea while keeping an eye on the two men. When Dorothea stopped sobbing, Wil checked the men for handguns, took their knives, gathered their rifles, and took them to the river and threw them in. He took the saddles and bridles off the buffalo hunters' horses, and slapped them on the rump. He then got on the gelding. Dorothea covered herself as best she could with the torn dress, and Wil helped her on behind him and turned to leave. The gut shot man said, "You can't leave us like this. Finish the job and kill us."

Wil looked at the man, threw one of the skinning knives within reach of the gut-shot man, and said, "You have your skinning knife; do as you think best. After what you intended for my wife, you get no favors from me." Wil and Dorothea walked the horse back to the wagons. Betty told Dorothea to lay down in the wagon and rest. She would fix supper. Other than bruises on her face, Dorothea was fine physically, but emotionally, she would be scared of everything that moved for several days. Slowly but surely, she calmed down over the ordeal and seemed to be her normal self.

****

Fort Collins was founded as a military outpost of the army in 1864 near the present day Laporte, Colorado. The fort was built during the Indian wars of the mid-1860s to provide some element of protection on the Overland mail route. Travelers crossing the country on the Overland Trail would camp near the fort and replenish their supplies. After severe rains, the fort was destroyed by the resulting flood. A new fort was erected downstream on the Cache La Poudre River. Settlers began arriving in the vicinity of the new fort immediately. The fort was decommissioned in 1867.

After the army withdrew from Fort Collins, the town of Fort Collins was established and saw a population boom in 1872 when dozens of farmers arrived and started raising crops south of the Old Town and fort.

****

The drive from Denver to Fort Collins had taken six days, and they crossed the Cache La Poudre River on May 30, 1875 and camped alongside Spring Creek. The Slant BB men selected a spot as far away from farms as they could find, apparently not far enough.

Bud rode to Fort Collins to purchase some coffee, wet his whistle a little, and get what information he could about the trail ahead.

As the group was setting up the camp, three farmers, armed with rifles rode up. The supposed leader, a small disagreeable looking specimen of a man who was probably in his fifties and looked like he had eaten a sour pickle, stopped his horse a few feet from the chuck wagon and without any greeting said, "This is homestead land, and you can't stay here."

Bill was sitting on a camp stool drinking a cup of coffee, didn't look up, and didn't respond. The man said, "Dammit, I'm talking to you."

"No, you're not talking; you're braying like a jackass. If you want to talk to me, show a little respect."

The man turned red in the face and obviously didn't appreciate being embarrassed in front of his friends. When he got control of his temper, he said, "Mister, I just told you; you can't stay here."

Bill looked at the man and said, "I'm tired, irritable, and not in the mood to argue with you. We are going to graze our cattle here this evening, spend the night, cross Spring Creek in the morning, and keep heading northwest."

The man was full of himself and said, "See that you are gone tomorrow. I don't want to come back."

"Little man, I assure you, you don't want to come back here. I won't be tired in the morning and might just pull you off that nag and teach you some manners. Now turn that horse around and get out of the camp."

The farmer glared at Bill for a few moments trying to decide if he wanted to push things any farther. As he gazed into Brubaker's eyes, he figured he had already said enough.

When Bud returned with the coffee, Sara told him about the confrontation with the farmers. He walked over to where Bill was sitting and said, "I can't leave you alone for a minute without you getting in trouble." With that, Bud had a good laugh. Bill didn't seem to see the humor in the visit by the farmers. The night passed by without further incident and everyone got a good night's rest.

The next morning they got the herd moving, crossed Spring Creek, and headed towards Wyoming Territory. With any luck they would be near Fort D. A. Russell, Wyoming, in fifteen to eighteen days.

Chapter 28

On July 5, 1867, General Grenville Dodge and his survey crew plotted the site now known as Cheyenne, Wyoming, which at that time was in the Dakota Territory and was later named the Wyoming Territory. The site was chosen to be the point at which the Union Pacific Railroad would cross Crow Creek, a tributary of the South Platte River. The settlement was named in honor of the Cheyenne Indian Tribe. The Union Pacific Railroad reached Cheyenne, Wyoming, on November 13, 1867. Fort D. A. Russell and a quartermaster depot were established in August 1867, about three miles west of the town.

****

The drive from Fort Collins, Colorado, to Cheyenne, Wyoming Territory, was only about forty-five miles, and the passage was through lush grasslands. Along the way, the Slant BB group would cross Lone Tree Creek and Duck Creek. The Slant BB drovers headed the herd out early on the morning of May 31, 1875.

It was late spring, and the days were still cool, with a nice breeze blowing most of the time. Even though the days were moderate, the steady incline was tough on the teams pulling the wagons. For the men, it felt pretty nice after being in Texas during the summers. Dorothea was becoming more and more like her old self, and the lingering terrifying memories of her ordeal with the buffalo hunters had subsided.

The group stopped and set up camp on Lone Tree Creek in northern Colorado. After supper, Wil got his bedroll and said that he and Dorothea were going to go and check on the cattle. Wil looked at Honks and said, "Would you mind checking the remuda before you turn in please?" Honks said he would be happy to check on the horses, and Wil and Dorothea disappeared into the darkness with Wil carrying his bedroll and rifle. Around midnight, Wil and Dorothea were laying under the stars talking in hushed tones about their future in Montana when they heard voices off to their left in the direction of the remuda. Wil asked Dorothea, "Can you get back to the camp by yourself?"

"Wil, I'm not a child. It's only a very short walk."

"Honey, when you get to the camp, wake up Bill or Bud and tell one of them we have company."

As Dorothea was walking towards the camp, an arm came from behind a large oak tree and grabbed her and a hand went over her mouth. A voice said, "You scream, and you will get your man killed." With that, the man began pulling her along into the copse of trees along the creek. In a few minutes Dorothea and the man were joined by another man who had one of the horses from the remuda in tow.

The second man said, "Some damn Nigger came up and I put a dent in his head with my pistol. If he hadn't stepped on a dead stick, he would have

187

had me. Let's get this horse saddled, walk the horses off, and get out of here."

Wil woke up with a splitting headache and was disorientated for a minute or so trying to understand what had happened. Once he regained his senses, he headed for the camp as fast as his legs could carry him, woke up Bill, and said, "Where's Dorothea? She was supposed to wake you or Bud."

Bill looked at Wil for a moment and said, "Wil, slow down and tell me what's going on." Wil explained about hearing the voices and sending Dorothea back to the camp to awaken him, his going to check on the remuda, and getting hit on the head. Bill went and woke up Bud and Honks and told them what had happened.

Honks said, "There just isn't much we can do before daylight. There's very little moonlight and we will just wander around. Even if we could follow them, they would hear us and hide."

Wil said, "But they got Dorothea."

Honks looked at Wil with sympathy and said, "I understand your feelings, but we can do nothing until daylight. Then we will get her back and deal with the horse thieves."

At first light, Bud and Honks saddled their horses and picked up the trail of the two men without difficulty. Wil wanted to come with them but was having trouble standing and focusing. Bill and Bud both told him to stay in the camp. They would take care of the situation.

The trail of the two men led along Lone Tree Creek and then took off into the grassland towards the west and the mountains. The men were riding fairly fast, but one of the horses was carrying double with a man and Dorothea which was slowing them down.

A bit after noon, Bud and Honks came to a small gorge caused by water runoff from the mountains and followed the hoof prints. They had gone perhaps two miles when they heard screaming, but it didn't sound like a woman's voice. They dismounted, pulled out their rifles, and eased along as quietly as possible. When they rounded a bend in the valley, they were staring at five Indians, two soldiers, and Dorothea. The two soldiers were on the ground but alive.

Bud and Honks walked towards the Indians, and Honks held up his hand signaling he meant them no harm. One of the Indians pointed at Dorothea and said, "Your woman?" Bud nodded and told Dorothea to come over to where he and Honks were standing. The Indian pointed at the two soldiers and said, "Your friends?"

Bud replied, "No, army deserters. They stole a horse and took the woman."

The Indians were Arapaho and hated the army because of the Sand Creek massacre eleven years before.

****

On February 8, 1861, Chief Black Kettle, along with some Arapahoe leaders, accepted a new settlement with the Federal government. The Indians ceded most of their land but secured a 600-square mile reservation and annuity payments. This was called the Treaty of Fort Wise. During the Civil War, there weren't sufficient supplies to feed the Indians on the reservation. Governor John Evans of the Colorado Territory moved Black Kettle and his tribe to Fort Lyon, Colorado, and gave them permission to hunt in the Sand Creek area. On November 29, 1864, Colonel John Chivington led a force of 675 Volunteer Colorado Cavalry that attacked and destroyed a village of Cheyenne and Arapaho in southeastern Colorado Territory. The cavalry hunted down, killed, and mutilated many women and children, none of whom were committing any offense.

****

The Arapaho who appeared to be the leader said, "What you do here?"

Bud replied, "We are driving cattle to Montana Territory."

The Arapaho asked, "You want soldiers?"

Bud looked at the two deserters who were scared to death and then at the Indian and said, "They stole a horse from me and would have raped the woman and probably killed her. Do with them as you will."

One of the soldiers looked at Bud and said, "We're white men. You can't leave us here. We were going to turn the woman loose as soon as we came upon white people. We just needed the horse."

Bud looked at the two soldiers and said, "Yes. Yes we can leave you to the Indians. You are deserters and evil men. You could have got away without taking the woman. Give me your names, and I will report your deaths at the next fort we come to. That's the best I can do for you. If this lady's husband wasn't nursing a head injury from your gun, what he would do to the two of you would make these Arapaho seem nice."

The soldier doing the talking said, "I'm Private Herman Smithers, and he's Private Michael Jones. We are from Fort Collins."

Bud scribbled the names down on a scrap of paper, looked at the Arapaho, and said, "I need the horse they stole for the lady to ride. Come to our camp, and I will have a steer staked out for you and your people." Honks didn't wait for a reply and walked over, took the reins of the Slant BB mustang, and helped Dorothea on the mount.

The Arapaho said, "We come." As Bud, Honks, and Dorothea rode off, they could hear the screams of the soldiers.

Dorothea looked at Bud and said, "The soldiers kept telling me they weren't going to hurt me. Those men were savages."

Bud smiled and replied, "Which ones, the soldiers or the Indians?"

When they got back to camp, Wil and Dorothea cried with tears of joy. Everyone in the camp was overjoyed by her return. This was the second time she had been abducted, and she had been less terrified this time because she felt certain she

191

would be rescued. The deserters seemed nice enough and told her they just took her so she wouldn't report the theft of the horse and they would have a few hours to escape.

Bill asked Bud what happened to the horse thieves, and his only response was, "They got pretty much what they deserved. I gave a steer away to the Arapaho. They will be here later today or tomorrow to get it."

The five Arapaho arrived just before sundown, and Honks had the steer on a tether line grazing beside the camp. The children were fascinated with the Indians.

The Arapaho who spoke some English said, "You can pass in peace." No one bothered to ask the Arapaho what they had done to or with the deserters. Some things are best left unknown. After losing family and friends at Sand Creek, the Arapaho certainly had every reason to hate the army and return their brutality.

The next morning the Slant BB headed the herd out towards Cheyenne, Wyoming Territory. Honks had been right. Keeping a few steers to give away was an excellent idea!

Dorothea was amazed at herself. She had been frightened. But somehow, she managed to stay relatively calm and at peace. She didn't think the men would hurt her and knew that her friends would come and save her. Sometimes, she wondered if being a slave wasn't a lot safer than life on the frontier, but at least here, she was free.

Chapter 29

The Slant BB arrived in Cheyenne, Wyoming, on June 5, 1875, without further incident and camped on Crow Creek outside of Fort D. A. Russell.

****

Fort D. A. Russell was established in 1867 as a frontier infantry and cavalry post serving as a supply depot and to provide protection for the transcontinental railroad construction crews. The original fort was built around an 800' x 1040' diamond shaped parade ground. The diamond shape of the fort was designed to provide more protection during the harsh winters. Troops from Fort D. A. Russell participated in the Sioux Indian Wars of the 1870s. Desertions from Fort D. A. Russell were endemic during the 1870s because of the low pay and isolation. Soldiers would simply leave the fort, change their name, and go to work for the railroad construction crews for much better pay and access to more liquor and prostitutes.

****

After getting the camp set up, Bill rode to the fort, talked to the commander and told him of the two deserters, Privates Michael Jones and Herman Smithers, who were undoubtedly killed by the Arapaho. After the fort commander had heard the entire story, he said, "Sounds like they got what they deserved. I will notify the commander of Fort Collins. Thanks for taking the time to give me the information. We have our own desertion problems here. I guess it is the boredom more than anything, and the lack of women doesn't help the situation."

Bill went back to the camp and ate supper. After getting the children settled in for the night, he took his bedroll, and he and Betty went out to check the herd. Between Bud and Sara, Wil and Dorothea, and Bill and Betty the herd got checked most every night. The next morning the Slant BB moved the herd out towards Fort Fetterman, Wyoming Territory.

Two days out of Fort D. A. Russell, a horrible thunder storm hit during the night with lightning which lit up the sky, rolling thunder, and then a torrential downpour. The frightened cattle scattered in every direction, and the drovers could do nothing to keep them bunched up. Finally, they just gave up and got out of the way so they wouldn't get trampled. The storm ended early in the morning, and the crew started working to round up the cattle at first light. By noon, they had found 123 of the 260 mixed breed stock and four of the five longhorns. They kept at it all day, and by nightfall had recovered 230 of the herd. Bill and Bud talked it over and decided to spend one more day trying to find the missing cattle and then leave with or without them. By the end of the second day, they had searched high and low and recovered sixteen more of the cattle, which meant there were still fourteen missing. They might find the remaining cattle and they might not. They had recovered three breeding bulls, so Bill and Bud decided to get the herd moving north. Losing fourteen cattle wasn't in their plans but at least no one was injured or killed when the cattle stampeded.

As near as he could figure, Bud thought it was about 140 miles from Fort D. A. Russell to Fort Fetterman. Without further problems, he figured about thirteen days on the trail to get to the fort. That left eleven days remaining.

After the third day on the trail, Honks rode up to Bill and said, "Captain, we are being shadowed by Indians; Cheyenne I think. They aren't close, but I have seen dust a couple times and a reflection in the distance, maybe off a rifle or some decoration."

"Honks, do you have a plan? Anything in particular you think we should do?"

Honks scratched his beard and replied, "I think we should double the guard on the herd at night. Other than that, all we can do is just bide our time and see what they have in mind. They may want to get farther away from Fort Russell before they do anything. I just don't know." Day after day, the Indians stayed out of sight for the most part but occasionally dust or the glint of the sun's reflection off some object would be seen. Three days out of Fort Fetterman, the waiting and anxiety was over as a group of Indians came slowly riding up to the camp during the late afternoon. Bill got the children into their wagon and made sure everyone was armed with a rifle and waited until the Indians arrived at the camp.

A splendid looking Indian stopped his companions, walked his horse into the camp, stopped his horse, and said, "My name is *Hevovitastamiutsto*, Whirlwind in your tongue. We are moving our village, and with the buffalo gone, we have nothing to eat. We hoped you would give us a cow to feed our people until we get to our new hunting grounds."

Bill introduced himself, "I am called Brubaker, and this is my partner Bud Baxter. We are driving our herd to Montana Territory to start a ranch there." Turning to Honks, Bill said, "Honks, cut them out one of the longhorns if you please."

Whirlwind smiled at Bill and said, "I thank you on behalf of my people. Perhaps we will meet again, and I can return your kindness."

"That would be nice but unnecessary. We don't want you or your people to go hungry and are happy to help. Go in peace."

The rest of the drive to Fort Fetterman went without incident until they got to within fifteen miles of the fort. Thunderclouds began gathering, and the temperature began to drop. After about an hour, a heavy drizzle began, and the temperature dropped into the low 40s. All the drovers went to the chuck wagon to get their slickers. The weather was just plain miserable. Betty, Dorothea, and Sara had no place to hide from the rain and bundled up as best they could and just kept on going. Late on the afternoon of June 27, 1875, wet and chilled to the bone, the Slant BB crew stopped and made camp by the North Platte River north of the fort. Rain was always the most irritating part of the trip. The ground got wet, the wagon wheels gathered mud, everything got damp and musky, and it was just plain miserable. To top it off, when they stopped they had to make camp on chilly, wet, and muddy terrain. Finding dry wood for camp and a cook fire was always a challenge. To make matters worse, the drovers had to try to get some sleep while lying in the mud. Such was the fun they were having as they neared Fort Fetterman.

****

Fort Fetterman was a wooden fort constructed in 1867 by the army on what was then the Great Plains frontier in Dakota Territory. The fort was located on the bluffs south of the North Platte River about eleven miles northwest of present-day Douglas, Wyoming. The fort served as a major base for the start of several military expeditions against warring Indian tribes. The main role of the troops at the fort was to protect American pioneers who were using the Bozeman Trail.

Fort Fetterman was established on July 19, 1867, by Companies A, C, H, and I of the 4th U.S. Infantry. The fort was named in honor of Captain William J. Fetterman who was killed in a battle with Indians near Fort Phil Kearny on December 21, 1866. A group of ten warriors, including Crazy Horse, lured a detachment of soldiers into an ambush against an overwhelming number of Lakota, Cheyenne, and Arapaho. All eighty-one men under the command of Captain Fetterman were killed by the Indians. At the

197

time, it was the worst military disaster by the army on the Great Plains. It wasn't to be the last defeat at the hands of combined Indian tribes.

Fort Fetterman was the northernmost military installation in the eastern part of Wyoming. Given its remote location, the post was not considered a desirable duty station. The winters were long and hard, the isolation and boredom challenging, and desertions by soldiers were frequent. Supplies had to be brought in by wagon from Fort Laramie which was to the southeast or from Medicine Bow Station by the railroad. Soldiers had to carry water up the steep bluffs from the river or nearby creek. The soil wasn't conducive to growing crops, so vegetables weren't available which made for more unrest on the part of the soldiers assigned to the fort.

****

Given Dorothea's experience with the two deserters, Bill gave orders that one of the men of the Slant BB was to be in the camp at all times, armed and ready if any of the soldiers decided to come to their camp and attempt to trifle with the women. Isolation could make good men go bad and bad man become much worse. All three women thanked Bill and said it would make them feel much safer. The pistols and rifles they had lying around at arm's reach also gave them comfort. All the precautions proved needless as the soldiers stayed in the fort or on their patrol duties. At any rate, none came near the camp.

Chapter 30

On April 30, 1803, the Louisiana Purchase Treaty was signed by representatives of the United States and France in Paris, France. The United States Senate ratified the treaty on October 20, 1803, and President Thomas Jefferson announced the treaty on July 4, 1803.

The purchase included much of the present-day United States between the Continental Divide and the Mississippi River. The Great Plains, including what is now Montana and comprising the Missouri River drainage, was a part of the purchase. The entire purchase cost the United States $15 million, which was three cents an acre.

The lands of the far distant Montana were mostly unknown and too remote for the federal government to exercise any meaningful control. When gold was discovered, the Montana Territory was organized out of the existing Idaho Territory by congress and signed into law by President Abraham Lincoln on May 26, 1864. The new territory included a portion of the Idaho Territory which had been acquired in the Oregon Treaty. The part of the Oregon Territory that became part of Montana was split off as part of the Washington Territory. The boundary between the Idaho Territory and the Montana Territory followed the Bitterroot Range. Later, there was a boundary change which moved the Flathead and Bitterroot valleys into the Montana Territory. The boundaries of Montana Territory then remained constant, and Montana was admitted to the Union as the 41st state on November 8, 1889.

Montana had thousands of acres of public land on which cattle could be grazed. Consequently, cattle from Texas were driven to Montana, and large cattle operations started. The Slant BB outfit was one of those ranches.

****

After the Slant BB got settled near Fort Fetterman, Wyoming, a young Lieutenant named Wilfred Smith rode into the camp and informed Bill that Colonel Joseph J. Reynolds, the post commander, sent his compliments, and asked Captain Brubaker to see him at his earliest convenience. Bill looked at the lieutenant and asked how the colonel knew his name. The lieutenant said he didn't know but suspected that he had been informed by one of the other forts at which the Slant BB had stopped. Bill thanked the lieutenant and said to tell the colonel he would see him once he attended to everything involved with settling in the herd.

Later that day, Bill visited Colonel Reynolds and found him most unpleasant. Colonel Reynolds greeted Bill by saying, "Captain, I sent for you more than three hours ago."

"Colonel, three hours ago I was soaking wet and trying to get my cattle settled in. I'm still wet and not a captain. I'm a civilian and have been for more than ten years. And when I was a Confederate officer, I was never at the beck and call of Union officers. I came to see you as a courtesy, not because I felt an obligation. You're on the verge of using that courtesy up."

"I think we got off on the wrong foot, Mr. Brubaker. I have an immediate problem, and it has made me a little testy I fear. Please accept my apologies, Sir. My Indian scouts have left the fort, and the Lakota Sioux are raiding homesteads, raping, and killing. I know your history as a scout and would like for you to lead a patrol to find the hostiles and eliminate them."

"Colonel Reynolds, I know little about Indians. My scouting was during the Civil War. I don't think I would be of any help to you. And besides that, I have a herd of cattle I am trying to get to Montana Territory in time to get shelters built for our families and drovers before winter sits in."

"Mr. Brubaker, I understand your reluctance. I don't need you for expertise in Indians. Just track them and keep my troopers from riding into an ambush. You should be gone no more than a week, ten days at the outside. If I send the troopers out without the benefit of a scout who can keep them informed of the Indians' location and movements, they won't last three days. And without your help, white settlers will continue to die." Bill said he would give him an answer the following morning.

Bill, Bud, and Honks discussed the situation and decided that one of them should go with the patrol. Honks spoke up and said, "I'm not keen to go, but I have experience scouting for the army and have hunted Indians, so I am the logical person for the job."

Bill was reluctant to allow Honks to take his place but couldn't argue with the logic. Since Bill was the one requested, he said he would go with Honks to the fort and see if the arrangement met with the approval of Colonel Reynolds.

Colonel Reynolds had heard of Honks Pickens and was pleased to have him guiding the patrol. Bill said, "Honks, we will take it slow and easy, so you should be able to catch up within a few days. I still don't feel right about this arrangement. The Montana Territory is to be our home, and we don't want to needlessly make enemies of the Sioux or other Indians." The understanding was that Honks would scout for the patrol but not be involved with any military action. Colonel Reynolds said he was fine with that, and Bill said, "Well then we have an understanding." Honks looked at the colonel and said he would be ready to leave at sunrise.

Honks and Bill got up before daylight and had a cup of coffee together. Bill wished him well, and Honks rode out to the fort. Lieutenant Smith and twelve troopers were standing by their horses when Honks arrived. Early on the morning of June 28, 1875, Honks Pickens, thirteen military men, and one pack horse headed out towards the west. After a half day in the saddle, Honks found tracks of several unshod horses headed southwest. Honks told Lieutenant Smith to keep the patrol at a walking march, and he would go ahead and see if he could determine where the hostiles were. About two hours later, Honks cut the trail of several unshod ponies and followed the tracks. Shortly before sundown, he found about twenty Indians in an arroyo settling in for the night.

Honks returned to the patrol and asked Lieutenant Smith how he wanted to proceed. The lieutenant said, "We will wait for daylight and charge into the camp."

"You're in charge of this operation, but if you charge into the camp some of your troopers are going to get shot. You hold the high ground. Why not wait for daylight and use your carbines to fire down on them and maybe get the odds a little more in your favor."

"We are cavalry. We charge. That is our battle plan." Honks just shook his head and walked off knowing that this was going to be a fiasco.

At first light, Lieutenant Smith and the troopers had their horses saddled and were ready to go. Lieutenant Smith turned to Honks and said, "You need to get your horse saddled, Mr. Pickens."

"Nope, I didn't sign on to get killed. I will give you supporting fire from the rim when you charge into the hostiles' camp. I will tell you one more time. You are going to get men killed by storming into that camp." Honks moved his ground cover to the edge of the rim, took out several cartridges, and laid them out for quick access and reloading if necessary and waited. He figured the distance to the hostiles at about 200 yards. Honks flipped the 300 to 500 yards sight up and figured he would use the 300 yard setting and fire a bit low. The angle shooting down made accuracy more difficult, but Honks was an excellent rifle shot.

In about ten minutes, Lieutenant Smith and his troopers came charging down the arroyo. The hostiles had heard them coming, were ready, had taken cover, and opened up with withering rifle fire. Honks cursed under his breath, took aim and dropped an Indian, then another, then another, but it was all to no avail. Smith's men shot six of the hostiles but got themselves shot up in the process before they withdrew and took cover. Seven of the hostiles were dead, two wounded, and the attack on the camp broke off in disarray. Smith and five troopers lay dead or dying on the arroyo floor. Honks continued to select targets and shot one more hostile. The remaining Indians got their wounded on horses and lit out down the arroyo.

Honks got on his horse and went down the trail into the arroyo and started checking the downed men. Lieutenant Smith was dead as were four of the troopers. The one trooper who was alive was in bad shape. The six remaining troopers came out of the rocks and started loading the dead soldiers on their horses and tied their hands to their boots under the horses. The wounded soldier died about an hour after they started back to the fort.

When they got back to the fort, Colonel Reynolds came out of his office and wanted a full report. Honks said, "There ain't much to report. Lieutenant Smith insisted on charging the hostiles' camp against my advice. He and some of the troopers got killed."

Colonel Reynolds asked, "Where were you?"

"On the rim, shooting Indians like I encouraged your lieutenant to deploy his troopers and do. Most of those hostiles could have been killed if he had followed my advice."

Colonel Reynolds said, "I think you were afraid to accompany Lieutenant Smith and the troopers."

"Colonel, I really don't give a damn what you think. I have spent several years of my life fighting Indians. I gave the shave tail lieutenant sound advice. You sent him out there knowing he didn't know come-here from sick-um about Indian fighting. He decided he knew best, and he got himself and five troopers killed. All that has been accomplished by your sending out a shave tail is dead troopers and my needlessly making enemies of the Sioux. We are done here, Colonel."

Colonel Reynold's report to the War Department explaining the engagement with the Lakota Sioux contained the thinly veiled accusation that army scout Honks Pickens was somehow responsible for the failure of the mission. When the War Department received the report, Colonel Brockert Givens read the report and told everyone who would listen that he knew Pickens from the Indian Wars in Texas and that he was an excellent tactician, understood the Indian, and couldn't have been the problem. In his opinion, the report had the smell of an officer attempting to cover his own hind end.

****

Joseph J. Reynolds participated in the Black Hills War and led the Big Horn Expedition out of Fort Fetterman, Wyoming, on March 1, 1876. On the morning of March 17, 1876, Reynolds led six companies (about 380 men) of the 2nd and 3rd U.S. Cavalry Regiments in an attack on a Northern Cheyenne and Lakota Sioux village on the Powder River. The Indians were camped on the west bank of the river in southeastern Montana Territory. After a five hour engagement, Reynolds suffered four killed, six wounded, and sixty-six suffering frostbite, and managed to kill or wound only a handful of hostiles. Reynolds withdrew his troops and retreated about twenty miles south.

Reynolds winter campaign of March 1876, ended in absolute failure, and he was later court-martialed under three charges. He was subsequently found guilty on all charges, suspended in rank, and forfeited pay for one year. The fiasco at Powder River was caused as much by poor planning and lack of information on the part of General Crook and his staff regarding the number of hostiles as the battle plan during the engagement. Joseph J. Reynolds resigned from the United States Army on June 25, 1877. Reynolds died on February 25, 1899 and was buried in Arlington National Cemetery.

Chapter 31

After Honks rode out of camp in the early morning darkness to scout for the army, Bill had waited for daybreak and then started the Slant BB herd north towards Montana Territory. Bill knew when Honks volunteered to scout he was more than capable of taking care of himself and finding the hostiles. The problem was Bill didn't trust Colonel Reynolds and figured the colonel would try to make Pickens the scapegoat if anything went wrong. And after Honks told of insulting Colonel Reynolds he knew the Slant BB could expect little assistance from Fort Fetterman if they were attacked by hostiles. Reynolds was the type of officer who would never admit that he had made a mistake or that an officer under his command had blundered due to lack of tactical experience and training and would seek some other person to blame.

Word had a way of spreading on the western frontier faster than a prairie fire. Most people would just pass the loss of the soldiers off as another of the army's blunders. Honks Pickens wasn't exactly a household name this far north. Unfortunately, the people who knew the entire truth were the Lakota Sioux. Charging into the hostile's camp in the arroyo had been a stupid move on the part of the long knives. Surely they should have known the Sioux would be waiting. The man on the rim of the hill was another matter and had known what he was doing and killed some of their braves. Putting two and two together, the Lakota Sioux leaders realized that the man who led the soldiers to the war party's camp had to be one of the men moving the cattle herd towards the north. Honks may have saved some settlers' lives by killing the three hostiles, but he also made enemies of the Lakota Sioux and Cheyenne. Now he had the Apache, Comanche, Lakota Sioux, and Cheyenne all wanting his scalp. Unfortunately for the Slant BB, the Lakota Sioux and Cheyenne wanted revenge for their dead at the hands of Honks and were committed to killing the people driving the cattle through their land.

Four days out of Fort Fetterman, Indians began shadowing the herd on the east and west side, about one-half mile off. Bill rode up beside Honks and asked him what the Indians were up to. Honks just shook his head and said, "I surely don't know, but I don't like the looks of it." The Indians continued shadowing the herd all day, never getting closer.

The next morning when the drovers began moving the cattle, Indians again started shadowing the herd as it moved north. Bill, Bud, and Honks got their heads together, and Bill decided he would ride out to the Indians on the east side and try to find out what they had up their sleeve. They still had longhorns to give away, maybe that would appease the Indians, and they would ride off. Bill rode out towards the Indians, and they stopped and waited for him to arrive. When Bill pulled up he said, "I am called Brubaker. Do any of you speak English?"

The Indian who seemed to be in charge replied, "I am called Two Moons. I speak a little English I learned at the reservation."

"What is it you want? Why are you riding beside our herd?"

"We want the man who led the long knives against our people at the arroyo. Six of our warriors were killed."

"I sent the man, so I am responsible. Six of the bluecoats were also killed that day. My man talked against charging your camp, but the young leader wouldn't listen and got himself and five of his men killed."

Two Moons responded, "Your man killed three braves. One was Cheyenne. You must die, or he must die. You are brave man to come to us. Come with us, and we will let the others live."

"My dying wouldn't be a long-term solution for my family. I can't do that."

"Then you all will die."

Bill looked at Two Moons and said, "We are not young pony soldiers who have never fought the Indian. We don't scare easily, and we don't use single shot rifles. We have guns that fire many times before we reload. Many of your warriors will die if you attack us. Some of your braves died; some of the soldiers died. It would be best if we gave you a beef cow, and you rode off." With that, Bill turned his horse and rode back to the herd and told Bud and Honks what the leader of the hostiles had said. They debated as to whether they should stay where they were and wait for the hostiles to attack or keep the herd moving. They decided the Indians would do whatever they planned to do whether they stopped or kept going so they decided to keep the herd moving. The drovers were told to keep the herd as closely packed as possible. All the adults had their rifles out, loaded, and close at hand.

****

Two Moons, *Ishaynishus* in his native Cheyenne, was one of the chiefs involved in the battle of Little Big Horn. After surrendering his Cheyenne band in 1877, Two Moons chose to enlist as an Indian scout for General Nelson A. Miles, the man to whom he had surrendered. As a result of Two Moons' pleasant personality, understanding, and friendliness towards the whites, he was appointed chief of the Cheyenne Northern Reservation.

Two Moons made several trips to Washington, D.C., to discuss the future of and lobby for the Northern Cheyenne people and encourage better conditions on the reservation. In 1914, Two Moons met with then President Woodrow Wilson to discuss matters regarding his people. Two Moons died of natural causes in 1917. His grave is located alongside U.S. Route 212, west of Busby, Montana. Two Moons' likeness can be seen on James Fraser's famous Buffalo nickel.

****

The day passed and nothing happened except the Indians kept shadowing the herd. They could count twelve Indians on each side of the herd. Even if there weren't others, they were outnumbered more than two to one. Everyone was getting more and more nervous. They knew the Indians were going to attack. They just didn't know when, or if the hostiles were waiting for more of their band to show up. Right before sundown the hostiles attacked from the west making it difficult to see them in the glare of the setting sun. Bill, Honks, Betty, and Fester started firing at the approaching hostiles. Bud, Wil, Sara, and the others got ready for an attack from the east. In the first two salvos, Bill's group took five of the hostiles out of their saddles, either killed or wounded. The bad news was that Duke was hit by a bullet and killed. For whatever reason Daisy, had never conceived, so there had never been pups. The Indians turned their ponies and headed back to the west. The hostiles on the eastern side never attacked. The Slant BB moved the wagons to form a triangle leaving as little gap as possible, lit a fire, and waited.

Under cover of darkness, the Indians on the western side led by Little Wolf retrieved their five dead and one injured brave. The six men walked their horses and led the mounts carrying the dead and wounded well shy of the camp and met up with the twelve hostiles on the east side of the herd which was led by Two Moons. Two Moons and Little Wolf discussed their situation and agreed that the people herding the cattle were great warriors. Even the women fought like devils. Little Wolf said, "My son

Dark Turtle is badly wounded. Without help he will die."

Two Moons said, "I will go to the white man called Brubaker's camp and see if he will help your son."

Little Wolf replied, "If you go into their camp, this Brubaker will kill you"

"I don't think so. A man with the courage of Brubaker will not kill an unarmed man." And with that, he handed his rifle to Little Wolf, mounted his pony, and walked the horse towards the Slant BB camp. When he got close to the camp, he hollered, "Brubaker."

Bill got up and walked to the edge of the wagons and said, "I'm here. What do you want?"

"Dark Turtle, one of my young warriors, was badly hurt by one of your bullets. His father wants to know if you have someone who can help him."

"You bring him, no one else, and we will do what we can." A short while later Two Moons led a horse carrying a young Indian draped over a horse into the camp. Wil and Honks helped the wounded boy off the horse and placed him on a ground cover they had ready.

Wil began examining the boy and found there was a bullet in his chest above his lung on the left hand side. He looked at Two Moons and said, "The bullet must come out, but I can promise you nothing. He has lost a lot of blood." Wil got his instruments and asked for lanterns for light to remove the bullet. After sterilizing the instruments in the camp fire, pouring whiskey over the wound, making an incision, using a retractor, and then a probe and forceps, he removed the bullet and handed it to Two Moons. Wil then sutured the incision and placed a bandage coated with salve over the wound. Betty brought warm broth and gave the boy sip after sip. After taking a bit of the broth and some water, the young Indian drifted off to sleep.

Bill looked at Two Moons and said, "The boy's father is welcome to come and stay with his son if he wishes. Just bring no weapons." Two Moons rode out of the camp mystified at how these white eyes could kill so proficiently and still show so much compassion. Within a half-hour or so, Little Wolf rode into the camp and dismounted. Bill led him to his son.

The next morning Dark Turtle was sitting up and eating some flapjacks with syrup. Little Wolf looked at Wil, pointed, and said, "Knife." Wil pulled out his knife and handed it to Little Wolf who opened a small gash on the palm of his right hand, pointed at Wil's right hand, and handed him back the knife. Wil got the gist of what Little Wolf wanted and slit the palm of his right hand and locked hands with the Indian.

Little Wolf said, "Fighting and dying is part of living on the plains. Kindness is not part of what we expect. We are now brothers. The Lakota Sioux and Northern Cheyenne will not bother you or your friends." He then looked sternly at Bill and said, "Our brothers do not help the pony soldiers kill us." Bill nodded his head in understanding, and nothing more was said. The Slant BB stayed in their camp for three days while Dark Turtle recovered enough so that he could ride a horse. The Indians rode away and waved as they went.

The Slant BB left with the herd the following morning, and fifteen days later, crossed the Little Powder River southeast of present day Broadus, Montana. They had arrived in Montana on the 8th day of July 1875. There was an abundance of grass as far as the eye could see, and Plum Creek and Annis Creek, which fed the Little Powder River, were within walking distance. They picked a site near Plum Creek and began the process of cutting timber for a corral, building three cabins, a bunkhouse, and work shed.

It was late summer. The nights were getting chilly. Winter wasn't far away, and they had a lot of work to accomplish before the freezing temperatures and snows arrived.

Chapter 32

It was the afternoon of the 13th of August 1875, and it was miserably hot. The men were all either working on the structures, tending to the cattle and horses, getting the recently completed tack shed organized, or out looking for strays. Mattie and BJ had gotten permission from their mother to go to Plum Creek to play in the water. The stream wasn't deep enough for swimming. Plum Creek was a 200 yard walk from the ranch complex and had a canopy of ponderosa pines along the bank on both sides of the stream. The five younger children were in the camp getting in the way, shrieking, laughing, and trying the patience of Sara and Betty.

After a couple hours, Sara thought it was time for BJ and Mattie to be back in the camp. She walked towards Plum Creek and hollered for them to come on back to the camp, supper was going to be ready in about thirty minutes. Sara didn't get any response and couldn't see them because of the undergrowth between the trees which lined the creek bank, so she walked on to the creek. BJ and Mattie were not there. She looked up and down the stream, no BJ and no Mattie. She yelled as loud as she could. No reply.

Sara ran as fast as she could to the structures the men were working on and hollered at Bud, "BJ and Mattie are gone." Bill came down the ladder from the roof of the main cabin, and Bud came running around from the rear of the kitchen which connected the two larger cabins. Bill and Bud ran to the creek and started walking around searching for some sign to help them determine what might have happened. After walking down the bank some yards, Bill found the hoof prints of three unshod horses. Bud came walking up holding a piece of cloth from Mattie's dress.

It was late afternoon, and neither Bill nor Bud was familiar with the area or the terrain beyond sight of the structures they were building. They had been too preoccupied with the building of living quarters to do any exploring. There was precious little time to find the direction of the trail and follow it before it would be dark. They ran to the corral. Each man saddled a horse, got their weapons, and told Honks he was in charge until they got back. They hugged their wives and assured them they would get the children back, headed to the creek, and started following the tracks which led due north. They had no idea what tribe of Indians they were dealing with or where they might take the children, so they could only follow the tracks and hope they didn't lose the trail.

The Indians were riding through tall grass and staying fairly close to Plum Creek. The grass made it difficult, but not impossible, to see where they had passed. Every place the three horses had passed, the grass was bent or crushed. The problem was, they had to go slow to be sure they didn't lose the trail. The sun set at 6:45 PM, and they went through a period of half-light. Then it got dark, and they had to stop and wait for the moon to expose itself. It was close to a full moon, and they could see well enough to slowly follow the indentations in the

216

grass. Stopping for the night wasn't an option because the longer they waited to follow the trail through the grass, the more the foliage would return to its natural state before the horses disturbed it. So they slowly and carefully pressed on.

They had no idea if or where the Indians would stop to spend the night. They just kept slowly riding and following the bent grass and the rare horse droppings. The horse apples were still fairly fresh, so they weren't very far behind the Indians. During the early morning, the grass land transitioned into a large canyon. They had been following the tracks for about ten hours and figured they had covered about forty miles. The terrain they were now headed into appeared to lead to the distant mountains. Other than dismounting to take care of bodily functions and water the horses a couple times from small streams, they had not stopped. They had just continued to follow the trail and hoped beyond hope they didn't lose sight of the tracks as they entered the mixture of rocks and hard-packed dirt.

Bill and Bud felt confident the Sioux or Cheyenne wouldn't have taken the children. They had given their word of friendship to the Slant BB. Of course, the Cheyenne and Sioux were large tribes, and some rogue band who didn't know about the Slant BB could be the culprits. The problem was Montana Territory was teeming with Indians. Arapaho, Crow, Kiowa, and Flathead (Salis), along with other smaller groups, lived or wandered through the southeastern part of the territory. The reality was that whoever took the children could belong to any of the tribes that wandered the Great Plains.

Around 9 AM on the 14th, Bill and Bud saw an Indian village in the distance next to the side of either a small river or large creek. There were about twenty teepees, several horses picketed, and dogs barking as they approached the village. The village was situated next to a sandstone formation which had a giant capstone on its top. The place would later be known as Crow Rock. As they got closer, Indians began coming out of teepees, from the creek where they had been bathing, and from the horses that were picketed just outside the village. Bill and Bud never slowed down or sped up and just walked their horses into the camp with their hands raised to indicate they were not a threat. A large brave walked up and grasped both horses' bridle, one in each hand and said, "Stop." The man looked similar to the Cheyenne they had helped on the prairie, but neither Bill nor Bud was an expert on Indians. Right then, they realized they should have brought Honks along. He had all the Indian knowledge.

Bill and Bud sat still on their horses, making sure their hands were well away from their weapons. In a couple minutes, Little Wolf walked up and said, "Brubaker, welcome, why do you visit me?"

Bill looked at the chief for a couple moments and replied, "Little Wolf, you told us that the Cheyenne and Sioux would be our friends. Yesterday, Indians took our two oldest children. Their tracks lead towards your camp. We lost the trail amongst all the pony tracks around your village."

Little Wolf looked at the man holding the horses' reins and, speaking in their native tongue, asked the man what he knew of the taking of Brubaker's children. Bill and Bud couldn't understand the words, but they knew from the reaction of the Indian holding the horses he was nervous when he responded.

Little Wolf looked at Bill and said, "Some young Kiowa braves took your children. They were on their way to their village up the canyon a few miles, stopped, and watered their horses here. A white boy and girl were with them. Gray Bear saw them but said nothing." With that, Little Wolf hollered at some of the Indians who were standing around and they ran for their horses. Within a couple minutes, Little Wolf and ten well-armed braves were mounted and ready to ride. Little Wolf led the procession up the canyon, and the group came upon the Kiowa village in about an hour.

When they entered the village, Little Wolf spoke to the Kiowa leader in a common language. The chief of the Kiowa called out in a loud voice. Three young braves, little more than boys really, appeared with BJ and Mattie in tow. The Kiowa chief struck the closest boy with the back of his hand and sent him sprawling on the ground. The other two boys backed away, leaving BJ and Mattie standing alone. Bill and Bud dismounted, and the children ran to their father, crying and scared to death. Other than a welt over BJ's right eye and a tear on Mattie's dress, the children seemed to be in good condition, at least physically.

Little Wolf spoke to the Kiowa chief, who in turn, spoke to the three boys who took off running. In a couple minutes, the boys returned with three ponies. Bill and Bud helped BJ and Mattie onto two of the Indian ponies and mounted their own horses. Little Wolf looked at Bill and said, "The boys punishment is that they will each lose their horse. Amongst the Kiowa, that is no small punishment. The three ponies now belong to the children." The chief, who was named White Bear in English, looked at Bill and Bud but spoke to Little Wolf who translated.

White Bear said, "I am sorry my braves took your children and caused you anguish. They will be punished. The Kiowa did not know of your friendship with Little Wolf and will not bother you again. You have my solemn word."

Bill looked at White Bear and said, "You have given us our children back. They are young and will forget their terror. You have my thanks and my friendship. You and your people are welcome to come to the Slant BB as you move your village south, and if we can help you, we will." Little Wolf translated. Bill reached out his hand to White Bear who took it, and both men nodded. Bud took the lead of the third pony, and they headed to Little Wolf's village.

Bill and Bud stopped at Little Wolf's village just long enough for them and the children to eat. Both men and the children were bone tired, but since they knew that Betty and Sara were frantic with worry. They left the village immediately after eating and thanking Little Wolf.

They held the tired horses to a slow canter and arrived at the Slant BB just before sunset. To say that Betty and Sara were overjoyed would be a gross understatement. After tears, hugs, and mothering, both children were tucked into bed.

The children had been lucky. Without the intervention of Little Wolf, it could have been a terrible tragedy. A lesson had been learned. The children were to stay within sight of their parents at all times, no exceptions other than when they needed to use the privy.

Bill and Bud slept like the dead and resumed the work on the structures when they woke up and had their coffee and some flapjacks. BJ and Mattie didn't suffer any long lasting trauma from their capture by the Indians and would have a story to tell their children and grandchildren. Nathan, Freddie, and Billy were already enthralled by BJ and Mattie's story of being taken by the Indians and their fathers' rescue of them. Mary and Carrie Brubaker were too young to understand what had happened.

****

White Bear (*Set'tainte*) and Lone Wolf (*Gui-pah-gho*) were two of the principal chiefs of the Kiowa Indian tribe. Both chiefs were respected and feared among Anglo settlers and other Indian tribes on the Great Plains. Both chiefs were reputed to have been involved in the Battle of Adobe Walls.

221

Although White Bear took no active role in the battle, he was sent to Huntsville Prison, Huntsville, Texas, where he committed suicide on October 11, 1878, by diving head-first from a high window of the prison hospital.

Lone Wolf contracted malaria during his imprisonment in the dungeons at Fort Marion, Saint Augustine, Florida. He was sent home in 1879 to live out his days. He died in July 1879. The death of Lone Wolf signaled the end of the war history of the Kiowa Indian tribe.

Chapter 33

For a place that was supposedly miserably cold in the winter, July 1875, was blistering hot in the southeastern part of the Montana Territory. The normal July temperature would be in the mid-80s during the day and drop into a pleasant mid-50s or low 60s at night, but not this summer. During the afternoons the temperature would rise into the mid-90s with a slight hot breeze which did nothing to make working outside more comfortable.

The Slant BB crew had a lot of work ahead of them in order to prepare for the harsh winters they had been told and read about. As early as October, temperatures could be in the 40s during the day and drop into the low 30s and sometimes the upper 20s at night.

The building programs were going well. Other than the taking of BJ and Mattie, there had been no trouble with the Indians, and that had turned out well. As August started to play out, it got even hotter and then started to cool down in early September. With the cooler weather, the work progressed at a quicker pace, and everyone was happier. Then the Slant BB folks began getting sick, very sick.

Sara was the first to get sick, and on the morning of September 17, she came down with a high fever, rapid heart rate, was extremely thirsty, suffered severe diarrhea, and muscle cramps. Wil came and sat with Sara and was trying to figure out what was afflicting her. As the day went on she became worse, and her skin became clammy and lost its elasticity. Bud ducked into the cabin every few minutes to check on Sara and asked Wil each time what was wrong with her. Right after noon, BJ came down with the same symptoms. Then as the day progressed, Mattie, Nathan, and Betty all started showing the same symptoms. Bill, Bud, and the drovers started having the squirts. Wil started to think it was cholera. He remembered that some of the slaves on the plantation he had lived on had come down with cholera, and their symptoms were the same as the Slant BB folks. They had yet to dig a well and were getting their drinking water from Plum Creek. The problem was the cattle were also drinking out of the creek and leaving feces in the stream.

****

Cholera is an infectious disease that causes severe watery diarrhea which can lead to dehydration and death if untreated. Cholera is caused by eating food or drinking water contaminated with a bacterium called *Vibrio cholerae.*

The treatment of cholera is relatively simple: drink lots of water, and the bacterial infection will normally go away. Unfortunately, if the water that is being forced into the sick individual is contaminated with the bacteria which initially caused the disease, the water intake only exacerbates the problem. Medical science regarding bacteria and its effects on the human body was in its infancy in the late 19th century. Bleeding, withholding fluids and other treatments which only worsened the condition of the patient, were the prescribed therapies of the day.

****

Having been involved in a cholera epidemic as a slave, Wil realized that the problem was water, and the cure was water. He had Bud and Bill draw buckets of water from Plum Creek, between dashes to the outhouse, had them boil the water for about five minutes, let it cool, and then had Sara and the other sick folks drink as much as they could possibly hold. He also told everyone not to drink any water that hadn't been boiled until they could dig a well.

In three days, all the sickness symptoms were gone, and everyone had fairly well recovered. After the treatment was over, Wil sat down with Bill and Bud and told them that it was his opinion that, in the short term, a well was more important than the buildings. Short of that, every drop of drinking water would need to be boiled for at least five minutes. The cattle had no other drinking source, and they would certainly continue to contaminate the creek.

Bill put two drovers on the well digging project, and within a week, they had fresh water. Bud helped build the framework to attach a pulley so that a rope could be used to lower a bucket, fill it with water, and then raise it to ground level. The drovers collected rocks to place beside the well hole to keep debris out and added sod as thatching, hopefully keeping any contaminated ground water out. Sara and the others had been mighty sick, but it was a learning experience and caused the Slant BB to take stock of the things that could kill them other than Indians. They were completely isolated, and other than Wil, completely without medical assistance if anyone got hurt or sick.

The next essential was to find someplace to buy supplies. They had plenty of beef; but coffee, salt, and other staples such as rice, wheat, and canned fruit had to be purchased. Bud had been told that there was a trading post to the southeast of their ranch and decided he would take a pack horse and see if he could find the place. He felt he knew the general location of the place and was confident he could find it, so he started out on the morning of September 22nd, after giving Sara and the kids a hug, promising to be back within a week.

The Sioux, Cheyenne, and now the Kiowa would leave those associated with the Slant BB alone. Or at least the ones who had been informed of the white men's friendship with the tribes would leave them alone. But there was always the possibility of some small group of the roaming Indians crossing trails with him.

Bud stopped at a small creek, filled his canteen, let the horses drink, and then picketed them so they could graze on the plentiful grass. He put his saddle against a tree, spread the horse blanket on the ground, and covered himself with another blanket and his slicker. It was going to be a chilly night. Just as dawn was breaking, the horses became terrified and then the pack horse was attacked by a Mountain Lion who leaped on its back and sank its fangs in the horse's neck. The frantic horses broke the tethers, the saddle horse ran off, and the pack horse was thrashing around and bleeding profusely. It had all happened so fast it took Bud a couple seconds to get his wits about him. He drew his Colt .45 and fired twice, hitting the cougar both times. With the second shot, the cat fell to the ground. Bud walked over to the pack horse and saw that its neck was torn open, and it was going to bleed to death, so he shot the animal in the head to relieve its suffering.

****

The Mountain Lion, also commonly known as Puma, Panther, or Cougar is a large felid native to the Americas. The large cat ranges from the Canadian Yukon to South America. It is the second-largest cat in the Americas after the Jaguar. The cougar is secretive and normally a solitary hunter. The cougar is more closely related to the domestic cat than any other species of the subfamily *Pantherinae*. They tend to hunt and attack in the late evening or early morning hours.

****

Bud had a problem. His pack horse was dead, and there was no telling how far his saddle horse had run before it stopped. He figured he had ridden about fifty miles from the Slant BB ranch when he had stopped to spend the night, and even though he didn't know exactly where the trading post was located, he figured it was closer than home. The problem was, he could wander around a long time on foot before finding the place.

After considering his options, Bud decided to attempt to find his horse. Walking out of the hills was iffy at best. After rolling up his blankets, slicker, and putting the horse halter in his saddle bags, he set out with the saddle on his shoulder following the tracks in search of the mount. In mid-afternoon, he rounded an outcrop of large rocks and saw his horse and two others picketed, but he saw no humans. As he gazed around Bud heard a voice from behind one of the rocks said, "You looking for something, Pilgrim?" With that an old man dressed in animal skins appeared holding a Hawken rifle and said, "From the smell of you, you must be a cattleman. Cattle stink."

****

The Hawken rifle is a muzzle-loading weapon built by the Hawken brothers. The rifle was used on the Great Plains and Rocky Mountains of the United States during the early frontier days. It was best known as the Mountain Man's gun. The weapon was developed in the 1820s and was eventually displaced by breechloaders and lever-action rifles.

The Hawken "plains rifle" was made by Jacob and Samuel Hawken in their shop in Saint Louis, Missouri, which was in operation from 1815 through 1858. The Hawken brothers did not mass-produce their rifles, but rather made each one by hand, one at a time. A number of famous men were said to have owned Hawken rifles: Jim Bridger, Kit Carson, Jedediah Strong Smith, and Theodore Roosevelt amongst others. The Hawken "Rocky Mountain" guns were typically .50 caliber, but since each one was made to order, some were .53 caliber but ranged as high as .68 caliber. They tended to have double triggers, the rear trigger being a "set" trigger. When the rear trigger was pulled, the hammer didn't fall but rather the action set the front trigger. The front trigger then became a "hair trigger," tripped with a light touch. In many examples, when the front trigger was used without using the rear "set" trigger, it required a firm pull, and others required the trigger to be set before the front trigger would drop the hammer at all. Even though there were more modern weapons, many ole timers continued to use the Hawken well into the early 20th century. In fact, Hawken replicas are used today in sport hunting.

****

Bud just stood there for a couple moments with his mouth hanging open and then said, "A cougar attacked my camp this morning and killed my pack horse. The horse you have picketed is my saddle horse."

The old man said, "Cougar, you say. I thought I had cleared all the catamounts out of these hills. Good eating, these catamounts. Best meat I ever ate. Well, sit down, Pilgrim, and have some coffee and a bite to eat."

229

While Bud was eating and drinking his coffee the old man said, "My name is Josiah Templeton and yourn is?"

Between bites Bud replied, "Bud Baxter. My partner and I have a cattle ranch west of here by Plum Creek. I was headed to a trading post around here somewhere."

Templeton looked at Bud and said, "I knew you worked cattle. You greenhorns couldn't find an outhouse in a rainstorm. I'm on my way to Brackerton's trading post to replenish my coffee, salt, and tobacco. You can tag along, if you like. He may have a horse for sale."

Bud looked at the old man and asked, "How long have you been out here?"

Templeton pointed to the mountains and said, "That there is where I have my shelter. I don't much like the low lands, too many peoples and too much rain. I came west in 49 to get away from the crowds. Was doin pretty good til you pilgrims started bringing cattle out here. Now I can't come out the hills without havin to be careful where I step."

Bud followed Templeton to the trading post, bought the supplies he needed, a pack horse for more than it was worth, well-worn panniers, said goodbye to the old mountain man, and set out for Plum Creek and the Slant BB. Bud never saw Templeton again. He heard stories of people seeing the man, but normally he just stayed in the mountains. The old man was strange and opinionated, but he had sure saved Bud's bacon. When he arrived back at the Slant BB, he sure had a tale to tell!

****

After the massacre at the Battle of the Little Bighorn, the U.S. Army began creating forts in eastern Montana including one where the north-flowing Tongue River joined the Yellowstone River. The fort was known as the Tongue River Cantonment or Tongue River Barracks and was founded on August 27, 1876. Another permanent fort was constructed on higher ground about two miles to the west of the Tongue and became Fort Keogh.

Fort Keogh was named after Captain Myles Keogh, whose horse, Comanche, was the lone survivor of Custer's command at Little Big Horn. General Nelson A. Miles made his headquarters at Fort Keogh. The first makeshift settlement near the fort was called Milestown, and the few residents made their living selling cheap whiskey to the soldiers. General Miles got tired of drunken soldiers and ran the settlers out of the territory. A second small town sprang up close to the fort in 1881 and was named Miles City in honor of the general.

****

Civilization had slowly but surely come to southeastern Montana. Bill or Bud could ride to Milestown on a one-day trip, leaving early in the morning, not dawdle in the settlement, and get back home before dark. The drovers found time to visit the little town to wet their whistle and sample the wares of the ladies who lived above the saloon. They seldom made it back until the early morning hours, ready to begin work at daybreak.

There was also now another ranch not more than thirty miles away which Bill, Bud, and their families would visit, and the Whitfield clan would return the visit, back and forth a couple times a year.

Chapter 34

After the shelters were completed, the Slant BB crew began the process of gathering firewood for the winter months. They had taken turns hunting game for smoking and to be made into jerked meat. Bill and Bud had been told that the winters would be harsh, but nothing could have prepared them for the frigid weather of the first winter. It was a daily job just keeping the snow cleared so that they could get out of the cabins, walk to the tack shed, privy, and the corral to feed the horses. The snow would accumulate, and then wind would blow it around and pile it at the most inconvenient places, like against the outhouse door. They had cut a fair amount of grass with hand sickles, let it cure, and then stacked it in the barn. Stalls had been made in the barn for the horses, but they could only accommodate six of the mounts. The six best steeds were stabled in the barn, and the remainder of the mounts just had to tough-it-out in the corral. The hay augmented the sparse amount of grass the cattle could uncover through the snow. The problem was, there were too many cattle to feed and too little hay. The Slant BB didn't lose any cattle the first winter, but they sure had some poor looking specimens come the final thaw.

There was little that could be done during the winter months but feed the fireplaces, stay wrapped up in blankets, try to keep the children occupied with games, and play cards. By Bud's reckoning, he had won all of Montana and a good portion of Wyoming in the poker games when the weather broke, and they could stop playing cards and get back to work.

It was early spring in 1876. The miles of prairie grass was green, and the different flowers were starting to bloom. The Slant BB cattle were beginning to calve, and the size of the herd would grow by about seventy percent in the next month or two. The cattle had survived the winter, were eating as much prairie grass as they could hold and were beginning to fill out. By mid-June, the herd had grown to 410, and of course, the three longhorns which they had left from the animals they kept to trade to the Indians for safe passage on the way to Montana.

BJ was almost six years old, and Bud decided to take an afternoon off from work around the ranch and take him fishing. He and BJ dug some worms, put them in an empty peach can, saddled two horses, and rode to the Little Powder River. When they got to the river, Bud cut two willow poles, affixed some thin line that Dorothea had woven from horsehair, and tied on fishing hooks. They caught a few trout and strung them on a small green limb with a fork Bud had fashioned to hold the fish.

While they were fishing Little Wolf and Dark Turtle and two other Indians rode up on the other side of the river and waved. Bud and BJ waived back, and the Indians crossed the river downstream so they wouldn't disturb the fishing, rode up, dismounted, sat, and talked for a time. Little Wolf commented that white men were entering their sacred land looking for gold, and he feared the friction between the miners and the Indians would end in war. Bud expressed his regret that the government hadn't kept its word to the Indians, and he too felt there was disaster on the horizon. Little Wolf, Dark Turtle, and Bud said their goodbyes, and the Sioux walked their horses back across the stream and rode off into the grassland. Neither Bud nor Little Wolf knew how prophetic their opinions were until the battle of the Greasy Grass on June 25, 1876.

****

In 1868, representatives of the U.S. government met with several leaders of the Lakota Sioux nation at Fort Laramie in the Wyoming Territory. During the meeting, the Treaty of Fort Laramie was signed by some of the Indian leaders who agreed to move to reservations. What the government didn't understand was that there was no central unified government within the Lakota Sioux Indian nation. The Lakota Sioux was a widespread tribe which shared a common culture, often was allied politically or militarily, but each chief or elder spoke only for his particular band, not for all the Lakota Sioux people. Consequently, the Lakota Sioux who signed the Treaty at Fort Laramie were only speaking for themselves and their followers, not the entire Lakota Sioux nation.

On November 26, 1868, Lieutenant Colonel George Armstrong Custer discovered a Cheyenne encampment near the Washita River, just outside present-day Cheyenne, Oklahoma. He made no attempt to identify which specific Cheyenne were in the village, ignored a white flag flying in clear sight, encircled the camp under cover of darkness, and attacked the sleeping Indians in the early morning hours. Within a short period of time, the village was destroyed, and the soldiers had killed 103 Cheyenne including the peaceful Black Kettle and several women and children. The non-threatening Indians' village was on the Indian reservation! The press and military hailed the attack as a wonderful victory. The Great Plains Indians knew it was an unprovoked cowardly massacre.

Many of the leaders like Sitting Bull and Crazy Horse refused to accept the treaty which actually worsened conditions between many Lakota Sioux and the government. In 1874, Lieutenant Colonel Custer was dispatched to explore a section of the Black Hills. A geologist on the expedition found gold, and when word of the discovery was leaked, it led to a flood of miners pouring into the Lakota Sioux and Northern Cheyenne territories in the Black Hills.

Realizing there was no method of combatting "gold fever," the government attempted to purchase the land from the Lakota Sioux, but again, there was no central individual to deal with. The Lakota Sioux felt the Black Hills was a sacred place. By mid-winter in 1875, the government gave the problem to the military to resolve.

****

In Mid-July 1876, Little Wolf, Dark Turtle, and several braves stopped at the Slant BB ranch shortly before sundown. Little Wolf dismounted and walked up to Bill's cabin. The rest of the Indians stood by their horses. Little Wolf asked about the boy and girl the Kiowa had captured, and after being assured they were fine; he turned his attention to other matters. Bill, Bud, Honks, and Wil sat on the porch, drinking their coffee, smoking their pipes, and listened intently as Little Wolf described the Battle of the Greasy Grass. The battle is better known as the Battle of Little Big Horn in which Colonel Custer and his entire group were killed by the Lakota Sioux, Northern Cheyenne, and Arapaho.

Little Wolf began by saying that members of the Lakota Sioux, Northern Cheyenne, and Arapaho tribes were camped on the Little Big Horn. They had gathered from distant reservations on the Missouri River in order for the chiefs of the various groups to discuss whether they should fight the long knives or move back to reservations. Some felt one way and some the other. Contrary to popular opinion, the Indians weren't gathered to make war. During the afternoon of June 25th, some of the Indians were swimming in the Little Big Horn, women were digging turnips, and the last thing on their mind was an attack by the long knives.

Without proper reconnaissance and without proper deployment of cavalry forces, Colonel Custer led part of his regiment towards the massive village to mount a surprise attack. According to some Indian accounts, Colonel Custer may have been the first casualty of the engagement as they claim he was shot as he forded the Little Big Horn River. If true, the soldiers supported his body on his horse and retreated. The Indians retaliated in a disorganized fashion and fought small groups of soldiers where they were encountered. Little Wolf said that some of the soldiers fought bravely, some threw down their rifles and ran, and soldiers' bodies were scattered all over the area for about a mile. As the afternoon wore on, George Armstrong Custer, his brothers Thomas and Boston, and a total of 210 members of the 7th Cavalry were killed by the more than 2,000 Indian braves from the village.

****

During the winter of 1876-77, Little Wolf and the starving Cheyenne bands surrendered to General Nelson Miles and were promised they would be moved to a reservation in their native lands. Once the surrender was concluded, Miles broke his word and moved Little Wolf and Dull Knife and their followers to a reservation in Indian (Oklahoma) Territory. By the summer of 1878, half the Cheyenne who lived on the reservation in Oklahoma were dead. Little Wolf and Dull Knife pleaded to be allowed to return to their homeland. Indian Agent John Miles refused. Ten young Cheyenne fled the reservation and Miles threatened to withdraw food until the boys returned to the reservation. Lone Wolf is quoted as saying, "Last night I saw children eating grass because they had no food. Will you take the grass away from them?"

Lone Wolf and Dull Knife led their followers from the reservation and repelled the half-hearted attempts by the army to capture them. They split their group in Nebraska, and Dull Knife took his band to the Red Cloud Reservation and surrendered. Lone Wolf led his band to the Sand Hills of Nebraska and hid. In March of 1879, Lone Wolf surrendered to General Miles, and he and his band were allowed to stay near their home on the Northern Plains.

Little Wolf later became a scout for General Nelson A. Miles. While drunk he shot and killed a fellow Indian named Starving Elk at a trading post on December 12, 1880. Little Wolf went into voluntary exile because of his disgrace. He was no longer a chief. He died on the Northern Cheyenne Indian Reservation in southeastern Montana in 1904.

****

The day following Little Wolf's visit a large patrol of cavalry rode up to the Slant BB complex, and the leader, Captain Benjamin Sparks, had his men dismount as he walked up to Bill and said, "Our scouts tell me a group of hostiles' tracks lead to your ranch. Have you had any problem?"

Bill looked at the Captain and said, "No, a small group of Cheyenne stopped by and told us about the battle of the Greasy Grass, but I wouldn't call them hostiles."

Captain Sparks looked hard at Bill and replied, "Why would hostiles stop at your ranch if not to kill you and burn you out?"

Bill smiled a knowing grin at the Captain and responded, "As I said, I wouldn't call them hostiles. The leader of the Cheyenne who visited us is named Little Wolf. My surgeon saved his son's life. The second reason is that we treat the Indians with respect and don't lie to them."

Captain Sparks huffed and said, "We don't take to white people who cotton to Indians."

"Didn't ask you to like me; didn't ask you to stop on my ranch. I tried to help your Colonel Reynolds by allowing Mr. Pickens to scout for one of his patrols. A shave tail lieutenant ignored his sage advice and got himself and five soldiers killed. No doubt Reynolds blamed Pickens when he filed his report to the War Department. Helping Reynolds darn near got my family and the rest of our group killed by the Sioux and Cheyenne. My people and I strive to live in peace with the Indians. Perhaps if the government, including the army would honor their commitments, rather than lying to the Indians, much of the killing would stop."

Captain Sparks told his troops to mount their horses and turned to Bill and said, "You'd better hope you don't need the army's help because it ain't coming."

Bill smiled and replied, "Captain Sparks, I have never depended on the Yankee army to do anything but lie, and I have rarely been disappointed. The only help I need from you, or the army is for you

240

to stay the hell away from our ranch. If I needed your help, I could grow a beard before you got here anyway." With that, Captain Sparks huffed, mounted his horse, and led the troopers away toward the northwest.

Chapter 35

By the spring of 1879, the Slant BB herd had grown to about 2,700 cattle. Bill and Bud decided to make a drive of 1,500 cattle to the railroad station in northern Wyoming. After cutting out all the nursing cows and calves, they checked the herd for brands, branded those which lacked the Slant BB imprinted in their hide, and started moving the cattle south. Bud's son BJ was almost nine years old and begged to go on the drive. Sara was adamant that the boy not go, but Bud said it was time for the boy to grow up some and get more involved in the cattle business. Sara wasn't happy at all, but BJ was going on the drive. Bill, Bud, and Wil to tend to the remuda; Dorothea to drive the chuck wagon and cook, and BJ, Josh Ramsey, and Daisy would go on the drive. Honks and the other hands would stay at the ranch, get the new calves branded, and provide protection for the women and children. BJ would be relegated to a safe position near his father at all times when moving the cattle.

Bud had bought a Model 1873 Winchester in Denver in the .38-40 caliber and had intended to give it to BJ on his tenth birthday. The .38-40 was a lighter load version of the .44-40 but still very effective up to 150 yards while having less "kick." Bud had taken it out a few times and allowed BJ to shoot and clean it. The boy was a natural at shooting a rifle. On a trail drive, every able-bodied person needed to be armed. When they were all saddled and ready to leave, Bud brought out a scabbard with the .38-40 inside and two boxes of ammunition and said, "BJ, if you are going on this drive, you need to be armed. Problems can find the young as well as adults." BJ beamed like it was the happiest day of his life. It was. The boy took the rifle out of the scabbard, loaded it, and put the remaining shells in his saddle bags and sat as tall as possible in the saddle.

On the early morning of April 17, 1879, the Slant BB drove the herd across the Little Powder River and made about twelve miles the first day. BJ was in hog's heaven until about noon; and then his butt started hurting, the chill of the air started to penetrate his body, and he began to realize this wasn't going to be quite as much fun as he had anticipated. To his credit, BJ never complained when his dad asked him how he was doing, but when they stopped that evening, he walked spraddle-legged and parked his hind end as close to the camp fire as he could. Bud got out some horse salve and told BJ to apply it where he was hurting. It helped, a little. Dorothea had bacon, beans, and biscuits baked in the Dutch oven for supper. Bud fixed BJ a cup of watered down coffee with a generous helping of sugar, and the boy was happy. He was part of the crew.

The drive proceeded on for three days without incident, and then the peaceful climate was disturbed by four men trying to cut the herd. Josh was riding the owl shift and saw three men who started cutting cattle. Josh could see them well in the moonlight, and fired his rifle, hitting one of the men, but he stayed in the saddle, hanging on to the saddle pommel for dear life as the three men rode off. Bill and Bud were immediately up and told BJ to get his rifle, stay in the camp, and watch for any activity to the north. With this admonition, they rode out to the herd. As dawn was breaking, a large man with wild hair and a filthy beard came up on a horse with his pistol drawn and stopped when he saw BJ standing by the chuck wagon with his rifle. Dorothea was hidden at the other end of the wagon with her rifle. The man gave an evil smirk and said, "What are you planning to do with that rifle, little boy?"

BJ was scared to death, but he was trying hard not to shake and replied, "My Pa told me to watch for riders coming from the north. I guess he expects me to shoot you."

The man laughed and said, "You probably are going to wet your pants, and you certainly ain't going to shoot me. I'm coming into the camp to clean out that chuck wagon. Put the rifle down, or I will shoot you."

BJ had his Winchester cocked, loosely aimed at the man, and moved the barrel a smidgen, and shot the rustler in his right shoulder, and the man's gun fell to the ground. BJ had the presence of mind to lever in another shell and kept the rifle pointed at the man.

The man screamed, "You little twerp. You shot me." He spurred his horse to ride down BJ who jumped behind the protection of a wagon wheel. Dorothea shot the man in the chest with her rifle, and he fell out of his saddle mortally wounded. When Bud heard the first shot from the camp, he spun his horse around and galloped towards the chuck wagon and then heard the second shot. The first shot had sounded like BJ's .38-40, but the second sounded like a big bore bullet. He was instantly afraid BJ had been killed.

When he slid to a stop in the camp, Dorothea was standing with her arm around the boy and telling him everything was all right. BJ was shaking and scared to death. Bud walked up and said, "What happened?" Dorothea told him how BJ had accounted for himself by wounding the rustler and then her shooting the man when he tried to ride BJ down. Bud patted BJ on the shoulder and said, "You did well. Shooting a man isn't an easy thing."

The other two rustlers and the wounded man had disappeared into the night. The next morning, Josh got a shovel out of the chuck wagon and began digging a grave. Bill read over the body after they placed it in the hole, and Josh covered the body with dirt. Bill put the man's rifle and gun belt in the chuck wagon.

Bill told Josh and Wil to look after the herd, BJ, and Dorothea, and they would be back in a couple days. Bill and Bud turned their horses, rode out to where the man had been shot, picked up the trail, and started in the direction the rustlers had ridden. Bill and Bud hated violence. They had seen enough killing during the Civil War to last them a lifetime. On the other hand, they knew that it would be some years before law and order reached the Montana Territory. If they allowed rustling to go unpunished, it would be a sign of weakness. Weakness in the far reaches of the west was a signal to the lawless in their midst that you were easy pickins.

Bill and Bud were able to follow the tracks of the horses without difficulty. They were traveling slowly because of their wounded associate and making frequent stops. Around mid-afternoon, Bill and Bud came to the Brayton trading post, located near present day Belle Creek, Montana Territory. There were three horses tied to the hitching rail in front of the building. Bill and Bud tied their horses to a small tree around the side of the building and surveyed the area. There was a rustic door on the rear of the building and an entrance door in front. When they walked cautiously up to the three horses, they saw that one had a fair amount of blood on the saddle.

Bill said he would take the front door, and Bud agreed to go in the back way. Bill gave Bud time to walk to the back of the building and then entered the front door. There was no Bud in sight. About that time, there was a crashing sound in the rear of the building, and Bud came walking out of a store room with pot, pans, and other goods rattling around at his feet. If it wasn't for the seriousness of the situation, Bill would have laughed out loud.

Seated in a corner were three men, one of which seemed a little green around the gills and slumped down in his chair. Bill pointed one of his Colt revolvers at the three men and told them to stand and ease their guns out of their holsters. Knowing that there were two guns trained on them, two of the men stood and cautiously took their revolvers from their holsters and let them drop to the floor. The third man tried to stand but fell sideways across his chair onto the floor. Bud told the two standing men to step back and then walked over and slipped the revolver out of the fallen man's holster. About that time, the store owner asked what Bill and Bud were doing. Bill looked at the man and said, "We're taking possession of three cattle rustlers. Keep your hands where I can see them, or you will lose more than three customers."

One of the rustlers said, "What have you two got in mind?"

Bill said, "We passed a large boxelder tree not far from here as we rode in. We intend to hang the three of you from it."

Bud spoke up and said, "No need to worry about the man on the floor. He's dead."

Bud tied the hands of the two men behind their backs, ushered the two rustlers out of the store, helped them mount their horses, and escorted them to the boxelder. When they arrived, they slipped a rope around each man's neck, looped the rope over a large boxelder limb, and then tied off the rope on the men's saddle pommels. Bill asked them if they had any final words or anyone they wanted notified. Both men declined. Bill slapped one horse on the rump, Bud the other. The men swung in the air with their bladders and bowels releasing. A hanging wasn't a pretty sight.

The rustlers were cut down, draped across their saddles, and taken back to Brayton's. Bill walked inside and told the owner, "There are two dead men outside to go with the one on the floor. You can have their gear. Just make sure they get a proper burial." With that, they got on their horses and rode off towards the herd. Hopefully, returning the bodies to Brayton's would serve two purposes: get the men a proper burial, and everyone who stopped at the trading post would hear the story of the hanging and know the Slant BB had no sense of humor where rustlers were concerned.

When they got back to the herd, BJ looked at Bud and asked, "Pa, did you find the men?"

Bud told the boy that they had and had taken care of the problem. There were no more questions.

When they arrived at the railroad loading area, two cattle buyers met them. Jason Smith made the first offer at $19.00 a head for the entire herd. Brad Bardwell spoke up and said, "I will go $19.50 a head."

Bill looked at Mr. Bardwell and asked, "For the entire herd?" Bardwell said that he didn't need the entire herd. Bill looked at Mr. Smith and said, "You have a deal. Give me $500.00 in cash and a bank note for the remainder. They had started out with exactly 1,500 head of cattle and the tally totaled up to 1,489, totaling: $28,291.00. The next morning, they met Mr. Smith, got the check, went to the telegraph office, and had the funds transferred to the Texas State Bank, Dallas, Texas. They took the $500.00 and bought supplies for the trip back to Montana. Bud looked at Bill and said, "I told you we would get rich in the cattle business, but not all of it came from Texas as we planned."

"Bud, if the market holds, we should be able to do this every couple years or so. We have about 1,000 head ready for breeding and another 500 or so that can be bred in 1880. We should be able to take even more to market in 1881." Bill and Bud now had $47,000.00 in the Texas State Bank, about $1,034,000.00 in today's funds. By late 19th century standards they were indeed wealthy men.

Chapter 36

Bill and Bud took herds to the Wyoming cattle market in 1881, 1883, 1885, and then sold all the remaining stock in the spring of 1886. BJ was now a seasoned hand being eleven, thirteen, and then fifteen on the four drives. Nathan went on the last three drives, Billy and Fred on the 1885 drive.

Mattie Lea wanted to go to formal school. She had learned everything that was available from the books her mother was able to acquire. Mattie was bright, and Bud and Sara made arrangements for her to attend the newly renamed University of Denver.

****

On March 3, 1864, former governor of the Colorado Territory, John Evans, founded the Colorado Seminary with the goal of helping civilize the new city of Denver which was at the time a mining camp. The school was founded as a Methodist institution and was renamed the University of Denver in 1880. It continues to hold the legal designation of Colorado Seminary.

Because of Denver's rough-and-tumble frontier town atmosphere, the school was relocated some seven miles south of the downtown area on land donated by Rufus Clark, a prosperous Colorado potato farmer.

Oberlin College, founded in 1833 in Oberlin, Ohio, was the first coeducational liberal arts college in the United States and the second oldest continuously operating coeducational institute of higher learning in the world. Following Oberlin's ground breaking decision to allow female students, other colleges slowly began allowing women to pursue their educational goals.

****

Mattie Lea drove the chuck wagon and cooked the meals for the drovers on the 1885 drive. She was used to hard work on the ranch, but feeding two hungry drovers, BJ, Nathan, Billy, and Fred, along with her father and Captain Brubaker was about all she could handle. The boys ate continuously, coming by the chuck wagon all day long to get a snack. No matter how much food she prepared, her brothers and the Brubaker boy still complained they were hungry. Her dad told her she was doing a fine job and to just ignore the complaints of the boys. Mattie didn't know it at the time but feeding the Slant BB crew was excellent preparation for the brood of children she was to have some years later.

Following the 1885 drive, Betty and Sara sat down with Bill and Bud and told them that they were ready to leave Montana. The isolation and rigors of fighting the elements was taking a toll on them. Their closest neighbors were more than thirty miles away. The children were fine as far as companionship since they had each other to play with, but they needed to be in a regular school. Mattie Lea was in Denver attending college, BJ was fifteen, Nathan fourteen,

Billy twelve, and Fred eleven. All were working cowboys when not attending Sara's classes. The twins, the youngest of the seven children, were eleven going on twelve years old. Mattie Lea was the only child who had ever attended a regular school. There were no churches, no towns, no civilization, and rare human contact with anyone outside their group. They had made all the money that they would ever need, so they saw no reason to continue living in the harsh and isolated environment.

Bill and Bud listened attentively and chewed on what their wives had told them. After talking it over, they agreed that they had amassed more money than they would ever spend and had far surpassed their childhood dream of being cattlemen. They had never really stopped and thought about their ranching adventure in Montana coming to an end. They just planned one season to the next. They mutually decided to sell out in 1887 and move to a town where the kids could attend school and their wives have a store, church, and freedom from worry about Indians or rustlers.

During the 1883 drive, Daisy took sick, rode in the chuck wagon for two days, and then died. Bill and Bud couldn't ever figure out what had happened, perhaps just old age. Daisy had been with them for nine years and was probably at least two years old when she joined the Slant BB crew. That would make her at least eleven and around eighty in human years.

Wil and Dorothea never had children, but not for the lack of trying. Dorothea got a sore throat in the summer of 1885. It continued to worsen, turned into scarlet fever, and she never recovered. She was buried on the ranch on July 17, 1885. Wil missed her terribly as did everyone on the ranch.

In April of 1886, Bill and Bud both had a feeling that the time was right to shut down their cattle operation even though it was a year earlier than they had planned. With the decision behind them, they sat down and talked the decision over with Betty and Sara. Neither of the wives had an objection. Once the decision was made, they started the process of closing down their ranching operation. It took close to a month to round up all the cattle, brand them, and get them organized for the drive to Wyoming. On May 14, 1886, they packed up lock, stock, and barrel and headed the entire herd and the entire Slant BB crew to Cheyenne, Wyoming, to the railhead.

The distance from their ranch between present day Broadus and Miles City, Montana, to Cheyenne, Wyoming, was about 330 miles. Under normal conditions, the trail drive would take about twenty-seven days. Because of the young calves, with several nursing, and still some cows calving, the trip would drag out for forty days. There was no reason to hurry, and the calves would be sold to ranchers to augment their herds and breeding stock.

The entire drive went without a hitch. The rivers were low, the Indians long gone to reservations in Oklahoma Territory, and rustlers had long since learned their health depended on staying away from the Slant BB. They arrived on July 4, 1886 and sold the last of their 1,304 mature cows for $18.35 a head:

$23,928.00 and change. Bill and Bud got $2,500.00 in cash to pay off the hands and buy supplies and wired the remainder to the Texas State Bank, Dallas, Texas. They now had a little more than $75,750.00 on deposit, about $1,705,000.00 in today's funds. Bud went to the Blazing R ranch, which was about fifteen miles outside Cheyenne, and made a deal to sell 300 calves to the ranch for $9.85 each: another $2,955.00 in their pockets.

Bill and Bud had paid all the Slant BB hands all their back wages after every cattle drive. The Baxter and Brubaker boys got the same amount on the trail drives as the grown men. At the end of the 1886 drive, Bill and Bud decided to give Wil, Honks, Dusty, and Josh a $500.00 bonus each in recognition of their years working on the ranches. None of the men were interested in staying in Cheyenne, so they decided to wait until the Baxter and Brubaker clans were ready to travel south and all go together.

****

The Slant BB had picked the perfect time to sell their stock and get out. The blazing hot summer of 1886 scorched the prairies, limiting the amount of grass available for cattle. When the snow started to fall in November 1886, most of the cattle were already starving and not physically ready for a harsh winter. The already emaciated livestock were then hit by a blizzard on January 9, 1887, covering much of the Great Plains in up to sixteen inches of snow. The whipping winds and temperatures of minus fifty degrees took a disastrous toll on livestock. The blizzard was catastrophic for ranchers with dead cattle lying all over the ranges, floating in the rivers, and even frozen to death in livestock shelters. The cattle that didn't die from the freezing temperatures died of starvation. Ninety percent of open range cattle lay on the prairie, the carcasses rotting where they fell. The horrible event was referred to as "The Great Die-Up," a macabre play on the term "round-up." After their catastrophic losses, ranchers stopped keeping such gigantic herds of cattle and began larger farming operations in order to grow food for the animals they had. Most also quit the open range where livestock could roam far from grain reserves in favor of smaller, fenced-in grazing territories. The winter of 1886-1887 signaled the beginning of the end to the days of roving cowboys and the untamed western wilderness.

****

Had Bill and Bud waited out the 1886 – 87 winter, they would have undoubtedly lost the majority of their herd and thousands of dollars. Sometimes luck is better than any other experience. Bill and Bud couldn't really put a finger on why they moved their leaving up by a year but were certainly happy that they had.

Their cattle operation in Montana had been a marvelous success by any measurement of accomplishment. Certainly, they had been extremely lucky having made friends with Indians who allowed them to live on the Great Plains without being molested. For the most part, sickness, accidents, and tragedy had avoided the Slant BB for all of the Montana years. Bill and Bud would have liked to have taken credit for their good fortune, but both the men knew it was mostly providential. They hoped good fortune would continue to favor them.

Chapter 37

After resting in Cheyenne for a few days, Bill, Bud, and their families started out for Denver, Colorado. Once the Slant BB folks got to Denver, Dusty, Josh, and Honks said their goodbyes and stayed in Colorado. Bill and Bud explored the town for three days and decided that it was still too wild and woolly to set down roots and raise their families. After they talked it over with Betty and Sarah, they mutually agreed that Denver wasn't where they wanted to put down new roots and raise their families. Other than lots of folks, it was probably more hazardous than Montana. They decided to go on to Dallas, Texas. Wil and Fester said if there was no objection, they would ride along and see how things shook out.

Shortly after the group arrived in Dallas, Wil made contact with a Dallas physician and got a job as a medical assistant. He was assigned the job of attending to the blacks who were seeking medical treatment. He did all the house calls and received a percentage of the medical income from the people he treated.

When they arrived in Dallas, Bill and Bud immediately started looking for land for sale. They struck a deal for two 200 acre tracts northwest of the town near the present day Dallas-Fort Worth International Airport. They hired carpenters to build homes on their properties, help with barns, stables, and tack sheds. Everyone in both families rode horses, and since it was the basic transportation for the period, corrals were essential. As much as they hated barbed wire, they realized that the few head of cattle they wanted to continue to breed, and sell would need to be contained. The free-range days around Dallas were over. They purchased several rolls of Glidden Steel Barb Wire from a Dallas supplier, had it loaded on a wagon, had pre-cut posts loaded on another wagon, and started the process of fencing the two properties. Fencing 400 acres was to be a formidable task. Holes for 2,400 to 2,500 posts would have to be dug by hand, the posts set, backfilled with dirt, and the two wires strung. Realizing they couldn't complete the entire undertaking with just four men, Bill and Bud hired a crew of laborers to do the bulk of the work.

Bill hired Fester to help with the small ranching operation, and Bud sent a wire to Denver offering Dusty a job. The wire found him after a couple days, and he headed for Dallas. Bill and Bud were engaged in the physical work along with the laborers, Fester and Dusty. They dug recesses and then placed bridge timbers in them to make cattle guards, a contraption that kept cattle and horses in. They had three gates built and erected on each property: one in the common fence between the two properties, and one on the west side of each property beside the cattle guard, to allow wagons, buggies, and horseback riders to come in and out of the ranch. They both had gates on the north side of their ranches. Bill and Bud had discussed the need for the gates beside the cattle guards. They decided the gates were good insurance against a horse breaking a leg crossing the timbers.

In late January 1887, all of the construction work was complete, and Bill and Bud had large signs erected over the cattle guards, one with Brubaker and the other Baxter, boldly proclaiming the owners of each small spread. They each purchased twelve head of Hereford cattle and one breeding bull each. The work complete, they settled in, but to do what, they weren't quite sure. As cattlemen, they wouldn't be happy without some cattle, but this certainly wasn't going to be a large operation. They would both be forty-seven years old in July. They were certainly no longer young whippersnappers, but far too young to sit on the front porch, whittle, and wait to grow old. They had lived on the frontier for most of their adult lives and had developed survival and hunting skills.

A New Yorker named Roosevelt had taken a hunting trip to the Badlands of Dakota in 1883 and wrote articles about the experience. In fact, Mr. Roosevelt was so impressed with the area that he purchased a small cattle ranch near where he had hunted. Roosevelt's articles, which appeared in several eastern papers, had caused a sudden interest in the west and hunting in general. And then Roosevelt's book, Hunting Trips of a Ranchman, 1885, stirred the imagination of many easterners. Bill and Bud decided to tap into that new interest.

On March 1, 1887, Bill and Bud founded the B & B Wilderness Guide Service, offering to take hunters and sightseers to Colorado, Wyoming, Dakota, or Montana to hunt bison, mountain lion, deer and elk, camp in the wilds, sightsee, and enjoy the Great Plains and Rocky Mountains. After sharing their plans with their wives, they took out advertisements in New York, New York; Boston, Massachusetts; Trenton, New Jersey; and Washington, D.C., newspapers. Within weeks, they had taken deposits for the entire period beginning May 1 and ending September 1 as the last trip of 1887. Bill and Bud coaxed Dusty and Fester into sharing the cooking duties and tending to the saddle horses and pack mules on the excursions. They each hired a Mexican man to help with the work around the ranches and a woman each to help with the house chores and cooking. There was a small bunk house beside the tack sheds on each property for Fester and Juan on the Brubaker spread and Dusty and Manuel on the Baxter ranch.

Bill and Bud had decided to alternate taking the hunters, greenhorns, and sightseers out on three week excursions. They would meet their customer(s) at a railroad depot of the client's choosing as long as it was on the route. When one man would be winding up a trip and coming back by rail, the other would be leaving Dallas by rail with horses, mules, and supplies in the livestock cars. Once the reservations and deposits started coming in, Bill and Bud realized they needed to make some purchases. Grizzly bear, mountain lions, and bison could kill a human in a matter of seconds or even with one thrust of a horn, slam of a paw, or fangs clamping on a neck. With that in mind, Bill rode to Fort Worth, Texas, met with a firearms dealer and ordered four Winchester Model

1876 carbines with the 22" barrel in .45.70 caliber. Since there were some inquiries as to whether they furnished rifles, and with safety in mind, he also ordered four Winchester Model 1885 falling block single shot rifles in .45.70 Sharps ST caliber. In the hands of an inexperienced hunter, the single shot rifle was safest. Both weapons would fire the .45-70 government ammunition.

The B & B Wilderness Guide Service had rules for the safety of their clients. No alcohol, no loaded guns unless in the field hunting, no straying away from camp without a guide present, and no contact with or feeding the wildlife. "I wonder where the momma bear is?" can be a terminal question.

Bill got the first trip, a Boston financial manager named Seth Rosenberg, his wife Margaret, and their two teenage daughters. The Rosenbergs had no interest in hunting but wanted to explore Yellowstone National Park which had opened March 1, 1872. Bill took Dusty on the first trip, met the Rosenbergs at the Dallas railroad depot, got them quartered in the Dallas House Hotel, and told them he would be picking them up at 7 AM sharp to catch the 8:00 o'clock train north. The outdoor adventure in the wilderness would start when the horses were unloaded from the train. The Rosenbergs were in the hotel lobby at 7 AM, bright eyed and ready for the adventure of their lives. When Bill and the Rosenbergs arrived at the train depot, Dusty had the horses, mules, panniers containing supplies, and weapons loaded into the livestock car. Bill got the Rosenbergs settled into the Pullman car. The

Rosenbergs had wanted to see the land north of Yellowstone, so after transferring trains in Denver, Colorado, and Billings, Montana, they arrived in Livingston, Montana, at the jumping off point. It would be about a fifty mile ride from Livingston to the northern edge of the new national park.

Early on, it became apparent that the Rosenberg girls, Mary Jane and Martha, had led a pampered life. When the girls were led to their horses, Mary Jane asked Dusty if it would be possible for him to give her horse a bath before they left because the animal smelled terrible. Dusty looked at the girl, smiled, and said, "Missy, you will smell just like the horse before this adventure is over. Might as well relax and enjoy the journey." They headed south, holding the horses to a walk, stopped frequently to rest, looked at the scenery and had a mid-day snack. About thirty miles south of Livingston, they made camp beside a small stream.

After Dusty got the saddles off the horses, panniers off the pack mules, and got the animals picketed, he and Bill set up two tents, one for the Rosenbergs parents and one for the girls. When Dusty had a campfire going, Bill suggested that the girls accompany him to the stream and see if they could catch fish for supper. Both girls thought that was a wonderful idea. Bill cut a couple small green limbs off a tree and attached some fishing line and hooks, put a cricket on each hook, flipped the lines into the creek, and handed the poles to the girls. He had hardly walked away when both girls had a fish on and were screaming for help. Dusty walked up and said, "You hooked em. You deal with em." Martha got her fish up on the bank, and Mary Jane managed to slip and fall into the stream but to her credit held onto the pole. Both girls were jumping around, and both said in unison, "Let's catch some more. Let's catch some more." To the delight of the girls, they caught enough trout for supper for six, and Dusty showed them how to clean the fish and then cook them. Bill walked back to the camp and visited with the Rosenbergs while the girls were fishing and answered their questions.

After supper and a couple cups of coffee, the Rosenberg clan retired to their tents to get some sleep. Bill and Dusty slept under the stars. Rising early, Dusty cooked up some bacon, beans, soaked some hardtack, and then heated it in a skillet. Everyone ate, had some coffee, and after Dusty and Bill got the horses and mules ready to travel, headed south. In mid-afternoon they arrived at Yellowstone and started their exploration of the hot springs and other sites. The Rosenbergs had rarely been out of Boston, and to say they were awestruck by the beauty of the Yellowstone Park would be an understatement. They stayed ten days in Yellowstone, camping, fishing, and gawking at the animals and then started out of the park. As they were ascending a moderate incline, a large grizzly bear walked out from behind a small outcrop of trees and stood in the trail not thirty feet in front of Bill who was on the lead horse. Bill immediately stopped the horse, pulled his Winchester out of the scabbard, and said loud enough for all to hear, "Get off your horses and try to keep the horse between you and the bear." About that time, the horses started rearing and the Rosenbergs were all on the ground. Horses were running away from the bear, and the Rosenbergs were frozen with fear.

Bill took charge and said, "Everyone start backing up. Don't turn your backs to the bear. Just walk slowly backwards, and for heaven's sake, don't run. Dusty, we don't want to kill this animal unless we must. Just keep your carbine on him, and let's see what happens." The bear stood on its back legs and roared. In a couple seconds, the bear came back down to all-fours, made a false charge, then backed up, made another false charge, and stopped. With the horses and mules going crazy, pots and pans bouncing and clanking around, the bear was probably as frightened as the people. Bill and Dusty kept their rifles aimed at the bear. After a few moments the bear just turned and walked back into the trees it had come out of. Dusty stayed where he was and kept his rifle aimed in the direction the bear had taken. Bill went to the Rosenbergs and checked to make sure they were all right after their fall. They all had wet spots on their garments, but he pretended not to notice. An up-close encounter with a 600 pound grizzly bear can scare the bejeebers out of ole timers who live in bear country.

Bill put the Rosenbergs on a train out of Denver to return to Boston. They thanked Bill and Dusty repeatedly and said it was an adventure they would never forget. The girls hugged Bill and Dusty and cried. Dusty looked at Mary Jane, smiled and winked, and said, "You don't smell as bad as the horse after all."

Chapter 38

The next client was the Jed Fuller family from Trenton, New Jersey. Jed and Frances had no children, but they brought their nephews Mark and Luke with them. They wanted to tour the Little Big Horn battlefield and then go into Yellowstone Park. Arrangements were made for Bud and Fester to meet them at the railroad station in Billings, Montana. The Fuller's impression of the massacre of Custer and his men was derived from the Remington painting which they had seen. They were amazed to see the reality of the battle was much different from what the famous painting suggested.

After touring the Little Big Horn battlefield, Bud took the Fullers to visit the Crow Reservation which is located in present day Big Horn County, Montana. Bud cautioned them it would be best to just look. Many of the Indians were still adapting to reservation life and still held a fair amount of animus towards Anglos. After touring the reservation, the Fullers asked if it would be possible to see the famous cattle country of southeastern Montana. Bud cautioned against the idea because the winter of 1886-87 had killed thousands of head of Great Plains cattle, and they would still be lying in the fields rotting in the sun.

Bud suggested that a ride to the Northern Cheyenne Indian Reservation might be more interesting. The Fullers thought that an outstanding idea and they headed towards the Tongue River in Southeastern Montana. Along the way, there were several dead cattle but not in the numbers Bud had anticipated, though that was more happenstance than anything because they missed the major ranches on the way to the reservation. When they arrived at the reservation, Bud found out where Little Wolf's teepee was located and went to visit with his old friend. Little Wolf, then a scout for the army, accompanied Bud to the Fullers and sat and talked with them and suffered their questions without complaint.

After the reservation visit, Bud took the Fullers back to Billings to catch the train east. The Fullers would tell the story of meeting one of the famous Indian chiefs who was involved in the Custer massacre the rest of their lives. They went east happily!

****

Betty and Sara got the children enrolled in a North Dallas school, and Juan and Manuel would alternate taking the kids to school each morning and retrieved them every afternoon in a Berlin, a four wheel carriage with a hood which could be employed in bad weather. Both men would carry a Greener shotgun in the boot just to be on the safe side. The days of roaming Indians and cutthroats were over, but with a carriage carrying pretty girls, one couldn't be too careful.

Betty and Sara got fine gardens going and planted flowers to make the ranch grounds more attractive. Life settled into a pleasant routine. Either

Bill or Bud would be at home while the other was out on an excursion with eastern clients. It was a comfort to the wives to know that one of their husbands was always around if they were needed in an emergency.

****

The final excursion of the 1887 season fell to Bud and Fester. They were meeting two husbands and wives in Helena, Montana, for a ten day hunt in what was to become the Nez Perce National Forest in 1908. Jonathan Smithers, with his wife Eleanor, and Frank Stiles, with his wife Janet walked off the train in Helena and seemed to be well-equipped for the hunt. Both men had fine looking firearms. Smithers had a Martini-Henry IV in the British .303 caliber, and Stiles had a Springfield model 1884 with a Buffington sight that fired the .45-70 500 grain cartridge. Obviously both men knew their firearms and had plenty of money to spend.

Both couples were good sports and pitched in to help with the saddling of the horses and setting up of the tents and camp in general when they stopped for the night. When they began hunting, they were southwest of what was to become Glacier National Park and northwest of Yellowstone Park. This area was without question one of the prime habitats for elk in the Rocky Mountain area. When asked, neither Eleanor nor Janet professed any interest in hunting. They just wanted to enjoy the beauty of the landscape.

Two days into the hunt, with Fester guiding Jon Smithers, the easterner harvested a fine bull elk at about 250 yards. Fester began skinning and quartering the carcass and drug the gut pile a few feet away from his work. Field dressed, the four quarters weighed about 300 pounds and were loaded on the pack mule along with the head that sported a fine rack of antlers. As Fester worked, he got a feeling that he was being watched. He didn't see animals or humans, but the feeling persisted.

When they got back to the camp, Fester mentioned to Bud the feeling that he was being watched while he was field dressing the elk. Frank Stiles was excited about getting his elk and couldn't wait to get started the next morning. After a supper of elk steak, beans, and skillet cooked hardtack, the group sat around talking about the day's hunt and drinking coffee. Around 10:00 PM, wolf howling started from all around the camp. Both Bud and Fester had heard wolves. They were, after all, a part of the wildlife in the Great Plains and Rockies, but they had never heard so many congregated in close proximity to humans. The howling continued for more than an hour. Bud looked at Fester and said, "Let's bring the horses and mules into the camp near the fire and ground tether them to the tent stakes. I don't like the sound of this." With that, they moved the livestock into the middle of the camp and added fuel to the fire.

The blazing hot summer of 1886 coupled with the harsh winter blizzards of 1886-87 had devastated livestock on the Great Plains, but it had also taken its toll on wildlife. Deer, antelope, and other animals either starved or froze to death. Unfortunately, the wolves survived. The first attack came shortly after midnight with at least four wolves leaping on the mule which was farthest from the fire. All the horses and mules were kicking and making lots of noise in their frantic attempt to get free of the wolves. Amidst all the confusion, Bud got a clear shot and killed one of the wolves, and the others ran away. Fester went and checked the mule and saw that it had some cuts on its skin but nothing serious. They added the remainder of the wood they had to the fire and kept watch.

About an hour before daybreak, the fire was dying down and the second attack came. Again, three or four wolves attacked the same mule, only this time neither Bud nor Fester could get a clear shot until the mule was on the ground and badly maimed. When the mule fell both Bud and Fester had clear shots and killed two more wolves.

Everyone was up, the men holding their rifles and the women standing as close to the fire as possible. Bud said to no one in particular, "Don't leave the camp. If you need to relieve yourself, we will look away. Wolves don't care anymore about humans than they do mules. I'm afraid this isn't over. Jon, you and Frank stand watch while Fester and I fetch some more firewood. If you see a wolf, shoot a wolf. Just be careful and don't hit a horse."

Bud stood guard with his rifle while Fester used his hatchet to cut saplings and knock dead limbs off trees when without warning a wolf came from behind a tree and grasped Fester's arm before Bud could shoot. Fester swung the hatchet and severed the wolf's spine, but he had a deep gash in his arm. He and Bud gathered up the wood he had dropped and went back to the camp. Bud examined the wound, flushed the site with some water, and bandaged his arm with gauze. Neither Bud nor Fester had ever seen wolves so aggressive. They figured it was a combination of too many wolves in one area and a lack of food. Whatever the cause, they had a problem. All the howling had brought more wolves to their location. They had no idea how many wolves were around the camp, but it was a bunch.

They were going to need more wood, so Bud had Fester stay in camp and asked Jon Smithers to take his rifle and stand guard while he gathered more firewood. After getting three arm loads of limbs, Bud figured they had enough for that night. For all practical purposes, the elk hunting trip was over or at least over until the wolves decided to leave, which wasn't likely. Bud fixed supper, and after everyone had eaten, they huddled around the fire and drank coffee.

As complete darkness closed in, the campers could see red eyes glowing in the dark from the light of the campfire. Bud and Fester had each brought three boxes of .45-70 ammunition and the twenty or so shells that were in their gun belts for their .45 revolvers. More than enough ammunition for normal conditions; but this wasn't normal.

Bud said, "Everyone, just stay real still. I'm going to try something." With that, he took aim at a pair of glowing eyes near the camp and fired and was rewarded by a wolf thrashing around for a few seconds, and then the sound of several wolves pouncing on the carcass and starting to tear it apart. Satisfied he had found a solution; he took careful aim and fired at a pair of eyes on the other side of the camp with the same results. They had now killed six wolves and fed several more with the dead wolf carcasses.

As the night wore on, more red eyes glistened in the reflection of the fire, and Bud shot three more wolves so the pack could feed on their remains. Fester and the clients dozed off during the night and woke up each time Bud fired his rifle. When the sun rose, the wolves were gone as were the remains of the dead animals. Eleanor and Janet proclaimed they had had all of the mountains they wanted and were ready to go home now. Bud took the Smithers and Stiles families to Helena and put them on the train headed back east. They thanked Bud and Fester for protecting them and waved as the train pulled out. Bud took Fester to a doctor in Helena, got the gash debrided, and a new dressing placed on the arm. They made it back to Dallas. Fester's arm healed fine, and the guide service prospered over the next several years.

The constant on all the excursions was the easterners asking about Indians, cattle rustlers, and ranching. Bud would always entertain his customers with yarns, some even true. Bill was more reserved and just provided facts. Starting with the 1908 guiding season, Bill and Bud turned the operation over to Fester and Dusty. At nearly seventy years old, they had enjoyed all the nights of sleeping on hard ground they wanted.

Chapter 39

BJ, with the benefit of his father's contacts and assistance, was accepted to West Point Military Academy as a cadet in 1888, class of 1892. Nathan followed his brother to West Point in the class of 1894. Both became career military officers. Both fought in the Spanish American War and World War I. William Huzzah, Bud's youngest son went to seminary school in Dallas and became a minister. After graduation, Mattie Lea taught at the Ashland School in Denver and made her home in the town. There she met a young doctor named Ned Swank at a soirée, fell in love with him, married, gave birth to, and raised five children.

Frederick William, Bill's only son, joined the Texas Rangers and served with distinction with that organization until his retirement. The Brubaker twins, Carrie and Mary, married brothers in Dallas: Carrie a deputy sheriff and Mary a rancher.

In August of 1900, a Western Union telegram was delivered to the Brubaker home. When Bill opened it and saw it was from a government office, he was filled with trepidation. Rarely does good news come from the government. As he read the wire, he discovered Theodore R. Roosevelt, the vice-presidential nominee of the Republican Party, was to arrive in Dallas, Texas, on September 3rd and wanted to meet with Bill Brubaker and Bud Baxter. Somehow, Roosevelt had discovered that their well-known guide service had been inspired by his 1885 novel "Hunting Trips of a Ranchman." Roosevelt had also discovered that the Slant BB had been one of the more successful ranching operations in Montana. Since Roosevelt owned a ranch, he was more than interested in their methods and stories of Montana.

Roosevelt and his entourage arrived on the train and were met by the mayor and several Dallas luminaries and were escorted to the Oriental Hotel. Roosevelt was to give a speech at the Downtown Club to a group of prominent Republicans that evening and asked to see Baxter and Brubaker before eating supper. Bill and Bud arrived at the Oriental and were escorted to Roosevelt's room where they were greeted warmly. Roosevelt grabbed Bud's hand and pumped it like a well pump and said, "I had the honor of having your two boys, Lieutenants James and Nathan Baxter, serve with me. They are fine men, and excellent officers, I'm sure you are proud of them." Roosevelt then turned to Bill, shook his hand, and said, "So you are the famous Captain Brubaker who scouted for Nathan Forrest during the Civil War. I had the honor of meeting General Forrest shortly before his death while I was on break from college and accompanied my father to Memphis, Tennessee. Forrest was a great military tactician."

Roosevelt, Bill, and Bud enjoyed a couple drinks together and swapped stories about their adventures in the west. Bill and Bud patiently answered questions about their time running the Slant BB ranching operation and their guide service. As the afternoon wore on, a frustrated little man stuck his head in the room and said, "Mr. Roosevelt, you must get ready for dinner and your speech, sir." Roosevelt ignored the man and kept talking. About an hour later, the same man stuck his head in the door, he was clearly nervous and agitated and said, "Really, sir, you must get ready. And there is no time left for dinner." Roosevelt turned to Bill and Bud and said, "I'm sorry, fellas, but I guess duty calls. I have thoroughly enjoyed our visit. If you ever have occasion to come to Washington, D.C., come and visit me."

****

On November 6, 1900, William McKinley was elected to his second term as President of the United States. His running mate was the young Governor of New York, Theodore R. (Teddy) Roosevelt. On September 6, 1901, while attending the Pan-American Exposition in Buffalo, New York, President McKinley was shot and died on September 14, 1901. T. R. (Teddy) Roosevelt became the 26th President, and youngest to serve in that capacity, at age forty-two. Roosevelt died on January 6, 1919, from complications no doubt caused by the tropical diseases he contracted during his travels.

****

Bill and Bud continued to breed Herefords and managed to come up with a polled (hornless) herd within a few years. The polled Hereford was prized because the breed was less dangerous to horses and humans who were working with them. The polled Hereford were not worth more on the slaughter market but were desirable and expensive for breeding stock. Bill and Bud, like the true innovators and risk takers they were, continued to breed polled Herefords and sell them well into the early 20th century, further establishing their bona fides as premier cattlemen.

Wil Byrd got septic poisoning from a deep cut he received from a carriage bumping into his leg and died on June 12, 1903. Wil had been an intricate part of Doctor Clarence Morton's practice for almost seventeen years. Hundreds of Dallas' black citizenry turned out for Wil's funeral. He had delivered babies, set broken bones, treated infections, and helped some of his impoverished patients financially. Bill, Bud, and their families were in attendance and mourned the loss of their old friend.

The Baxters and Brubakers continued to meet often for dinner and attended social functions, often as a group. Both contributed enough money to hold considerable sway in Dallas politics but had no interest in holding public office. Bill suffered a massive stroke on June 7, 1913, while eating breakfast and died later that afternoon. Bud had been fishing on Turtle Creek, which empties into the Trinity River, when Bill died. When he returned home and received the news, he suffered a heart attack and died. The lifelong friends who were born an hour apart in 1840 died an hour apart, just a few days before their seventy-third birthdays.

Betty and Sara continued to live in Dallas until their deaths. Sara volunteered as a mentor to school children, and Betty busied herself in different charities. Sara died in 1917 and Betty in 1921.

The two farm boys from the Huzzah had lived their dreams of becoming cattlemen. They saw their sons become quality men and their daughters fine women. Who could ask for more.

The Texican

Chapter 1

The rider was tired, dead tired and chilled to the bone. The severe cold wave and blizzard of January 14, 1888 had dropped the temperature to -5 degrees. He had been riding for hours in the blowing snow, freezing rain, and sub-zero temperature. Even though he hated to be in a lower elevation because it robbed him of the ability to see approaching danger, in the gale he couldn't see much anyway, so he decided to go into a narrow arroyo to get some shelter from the elements. As he leaned to dismount on the left side of his horse a bullet creased his neck. All in one fluid motion, he rolled off the horse and pulled his rifle out of its scabbard. He rolled to the side of the arroyo which the shot would have had to come from and made himself as small as possible against the side of the rock face. Whoever shot at him had missed, almost, but it was only luck that he was alive. Had he been upright in the saddle, his brains would be decorating the arroyo wall. He dabbed at his neck and found it was seeping blood but nothing to really worry about, just a scratch really. Now, the question was: who had shot at him, where was he located, and was there more than one shooter?

The man's name was Alowishus Winfield (Honks) Pickens. Pickens was the product of an Anglo father and Mexican mother and had grown up near Galveston Island where his father was employed as a carpenter repairing ships at the port. Honks was born on June 9, 1829, the only child of William Albert and Juanita Marie Pickens. The day Honks was born his father was drinking with friends and thought it funny to give his son the outrageous handle of Alowishus. The problem was, once recorded, it was his name for life. The given name of Winfield was in honor of General Winfield Scott of the War of 1812 fame. William Pickens had been a young private during the war and idolized General Scott. When Honks was a child, he tended to make a honking sound when he laughed, and his playmates made fun of him and called him Honks. The nickname stuck, and Honks liked it much better than Alowishus.

Honks was a medium sized man, about 5' 10" in height, thin, with graying hair and moustache. He was wearing a slouch hat, mackinaw coat with a slicker layered over the coat, well-worn boots, and heavy black tweed pants. Honks eyes were the feature that set him apart. They were dark blue and unwavering. When he looked at a man, it seemed he could see into his soul. His stare was unsettling to say the least.....

The Texican should be in print in 2019 and will be available in Kindle, paperback, and audio book formats.

Bill Shuey is the author of several books and the weekly ObverseView column. He travels extensively in his Recreational Vehicle with his wife Gloria and his fly rods.

He can be contacted at: billshueybooks@gmail.com
or at his website: www.billshueybooks.com

Made in the USA
Columbia, SC
21 September 2022

67074064R00154